With My
Compliments

Mark You

FORESHORE
publishing

Tec: 07975 583160

MARK HOWARD grew up in the small West Sussex village of Cocking in the 1970s. As a child, he was a daydreamer with a vivid imagination, a superstitious mother, and fears of what lay within the darkness and a passion to tell stories. His mother's fearful beliefs still see him salute a lone magpie to ward off a sinister omen. He spent thirty years working in photography and visual media. He is married to Yvonne and has two grown up children and now lives in Littlehampton. Blackthorn Hill is his debut novel.

DEDICATED to my wife Yvonne and my two children, Isaac and Ebony. And not to forget the invisible thing that followed me up the stairs at night when I was small. Inspiration can come from both love and fear, so thank you all.

MARK HOWARD

BLACKTHORN HILL

FORESHORE PUBLISHING
London

Published by Foreshore Publishing 2022.
The home of quality short fiction.
Copyright © Mark Howard 2022

Foreshore Publishing
The Forge 397-411 Westferry
Road, Isle of Dogs, London, E143AE

Foreshore Publishing Limited Reg. No. 13358650
ISBN 978-1-9168790-8-9

www.foreshorepublishing.com

The beginning of the end.

I

Ⓖ❧

I frantically ripped and twisted the pages from the pile of weekly Odeon & Herald newspapers. This week's unread copy sat on top, the headline "Hollywood actress Helen Flint dies after being hit by car." A striking studio shot of Miss Flint filled most of the page, the remainder dedicated to what I'm sure would be a sensational read, but the need for a fire was a matter of urgency, and the thruppence-priced weekly was a poor excuse for a newspaper, read or unread, its destiny was usually the firegrate and fragile Father Ambrose was in great need of immediate warmth. He actually looked blue with the cold, as if he had absorbed the bitter night time elements on his foolish quest. I couldn't help thinking it would be his picture on the front page of next week's Odeon & Herald,

"Foolish local priest dies at ripe old age of one hundred after spending night on hillside."

The paper`s signature style was always drama over empathy. We did keep a few copies; Yuri Gagarin first man in space in 1961, I think? The sad story and death of Hollywood actress Margaret Sullavan, a suspected overdose and suicide. Father Ambrose was convinced she was the absolute spitting image of his mother, who had died some eighty odd years ago, he was only fifteen at the time. He had no photos of her, so he bought an extra few copies and framed the cover of the elegant Miss Sullavan, his mother's double, and hung it in the study so he would never fail to remember her face. He described his mother as vibrant, warm and loving, and his father as narcissistic and violent. The subject of his father never came up that often, but it was obvious his early life was hard and at times brutal. On reading the article of Miss Sullavan's demise, he cried, something I had never seen him do in all my years as his housekeeper and something I shall not forget. The kindling was now in full blaze and the heat started to circulate around the room. Father Ambrose woke in a panic, and seemed very shocked that he was still with us in flesh and blood. I managed to calm him, I built the fire up some more and made some tea, fixed his pillows and sat him up. I explained that he was very lucky to be alive and if it were not for his vestment, and thick but well-worn argyle jumper he always wore under his similarly well-worn cassock, hypothermia would have got the better of him. But he was weaker than I had ever seen him. I sat and helped him drink his second cup of tea and steadied his hands.

"I can manage Mrs Hawkins; you need not fret so." His voice was frail, his words wavered nervously without control and for the second time in our near forty year acquaintance, a single tear ran down his cheek. We both knew he had cheated death and that it would not be long before it came calling a second time. He instructed me to call Father Martin and to do so with great haste, his only wish, to continue their conversation from the day before. Today, Sunday September 17th, 1967, would start the same, with the arrival of Father Martin and with a somber feeling in my heart it would end with the passing of my dear Father Ambrose.

It was now a quarter past nine, Father Martin was much earlier than expected. I had just put the phone down to him a few moments earlier, or so it seemed. I watched as he hastily made his way up the path to the rectory, his tall imposing stature and immaculate presentation as a man of the cloth instilled an instant feeling of comfort, and the mellow resonance of his voice could warm the coldest hearts of the faithless and fallen. He was a priest who truly believed what he preached, unlike Father Ambrose, who believed his guidance and Christian understanding should only extend to those that needed it most, he had no time for the token Christians, as he called them.

They had first met back in 1930, Father Ambrose had mentored the young Father Martin into a pastoral role at the church of St John the Evangelist in the borough of Islington, central London, his own parish of ten years. He was relinquishing his daily duties along with a dwindling congregation, and his role as religious counsellor at HMP Pentonville. Those that could fall no lower needed God so much more than his so-called token Christians, however, after Father Ambrose left St Johns, the bishop ceased all church assistance to Pentonville, believing prisons were the breeding ground of the worst kind of sinner, and no priest would ever change that. From the day he left London their friendship has been a near forty year constant, either by written correspondence, or a visit every few years. London seems a million miles from our little village in the middle of nowhere, and, as of late, Father Ambrose's arthritis limits his writing and his walking any great distance, so the telephone has been a Godsend, no pun intended. Although they are very different priests Father Martin knows there is more that connects them than divides them, so I was glad he was here and for the second time in less than twelve hours.

"Good morning Father and bless you for coming so promptly."

"Good morning Mrs Hawkins, think nothing of it, I feel partly to blame for Father Ambrose's condition, how is he?"

"Weak, very weak."

"He was most assertive yesterday in all our interactions."

"More so than normal Father?"

"Yes, he left me with quite a chronicle of events yesterday evening, unnerving enough that I didn't question his desire to sit out alone on the hill to watch the sunset, you know how stubborn he can be. I should have known from our conversation that he was not in his right mind. I let his words shock me to a point that I had to question what I was hearing, and in a weak moment I did seek to part with his company. I let my function as a priest cloud my judgement as a friend."

"Well, whatever you spoke of Father, I believe he continued to tell old Ben Foster who found him at around three a.m. sitting against the rectory wall, mumbling and shivering. He helped him down to the house and sat him in the study. When I arrived he was fast asleep, shivering and still mumbling in his sleep. Dr Davies arrived around nine and helped me get him to bed, the prognosis, he is fine mentally, but physically everything is failing. He is most insistent that he finishes what he started yesterday, so I beg you father let him get off whatever is on his chest without too much interaction."

I led Father Martin through to the bedroom and stoked the fire. Father Ambrose now appeared more alert and had regained some of his natural colour and I could see a small degree of his old self. I knew he would find the strength to talk but for how long would be another matter.

"Good morning Father Ambrose."

"Good morning my friend, please take a seat and make yourself comfortable, time is not on my side. Yesterday I told you the end of the story and now I must tell the beginning."

"Yesterday was truly a revelation Father, and not only because you were one hundred. Your story, which as yet, I have not processed fully, I must admit shocked me to the core. I will extend to you all the time you need and offer my guidance as a priest and more importantly today as a friend, I believe we could both benefit from some closure on yesterday's events."

"With all due respect Father Martin, my dear, dear friend, I am dying, all I require are your ears and undivided attention."

Father Ambrose then removed the small leather-bound bible I'd deliberately placed in his right hand, sliding it onto the bedside cabinet, drank the last of his now cold tea, placed the cup on top of the bible, and asked me to come and join them. I was reluctant at first, but knowing it could be the last time I would be of use to him, I agreed, and pulled up a chair near the bed, he took a deep breath and began to conclude the previous day`s conversation.

"As you know Father, September 1922 saw my ordination as Father Ambrose."

"Yes, I remember vaguely. I had just become a seminarian at the Corpus Christi Catholic Church."

"The bishop had for the first time in my three years of study given me permission to receive those who wished forgiveness at the confessional. I would listen and at times in consternation, these were not just sins, in many cases they were crimes."

"It is not for us to judge Father; I am sure you gave penance where it was necessary."

"Yes, yes, that's by the by, please, please refrain from interrupting."

"Sorry Father."

"So, a few days in a gentlemen entered my confessional box, he confessed to the crime of murder, which he had not yet committed. He gave no names and there was no remorse in his voice. Instead of `forgive me Father for I have sinned` he began to tell me a story. I of course informed him that I could only receive his confession to which he replied.

"I shall confess Father, once I have committed my sinful act of murder, which will commence, when and only when you have heard my story."

"I was unsure at first, but I soon realised I knew this voice, which makes no difference in the eyes of God, a confession is a confession, I could not disclose the chilling story that was to follow or his sincere pledge to commit a murder."

"I'm not sure you should be telling me this Father, you are still bound by the seal of confession."

Father Ambrose's hands twitched as if shocked by a small electrical charge and he shouted. "If I can't tell you, then who can I tell, you're a bloody priest!"

"Father Ambrose, please, must you continue?"

"That I must. I failed to put this story in front of the police forty-five years ago for fear of ..."

"Excommunication?"

"No Father, for fear that it was true and that we are all doomed, in this life and the next. A few days had passed, the gentleman would arrive, early morning, sometimes before and sometimes just after Mass. I instructed him to attend confession at odd hours, this way he could continue his story without time constraints. After about a week of attending, it was obvious that he was not alone in the confessional box.

"My son within these hallowed walls your confession is an act of trust between me, you and God and God alone shall give penance and forgive, whoever is with you, must leave."

"Father, I swear I am alone in here and in all matters concerning this story, and when I commit my sin I shall also be alone."

The few inches between the screen that separated us was not only small enough for me to hear the muffled but fitful breathing of a second person, but I could also smell a sickly sour scent, it was faint but very familiar. I did not press him further as I knew his daily visit had not gone unnoticed by the bishop. I was instructed to give penance and absolve him if I deemed it fit to do so and then instruct the gentleman to make restitution before his next visit, the bishop was quite clear on confessional edict.

"It is the failure of the priest if a sinner should seek confession every day."

And with this I knew the end of my term at the confessional box was imminent, at this point he had recounted a good portion of his story, but no confession. His crime of murder prescribed but not yet fulfilled, I informed him I would not be present to hear his story end.

When that session was over, he pushed a leather wallet stuffed with loose pages under the curtain, attached to the handle was a tailor's price tag that read, "Ten o'clock tonight, the Britannia Inn, Whitechapel, please be there father."

"I don't know what compelled me to do it, but a few seconds after he left the confessional box I stepped out and watched this elegantly dressed man walk away, and fixed within my mind then as it is now the terrifying dark and faceless entity that followed him out. It was of a physical form in long dark clothing. If fear was not in play I could have almost touched it, their motions synchronised, as if connected by flesh, every step in perfect time, and as he slowly walked away it mocked his every movement.

"As he reached the door he, they, turned and looked back toward me. I did know him and from the very first page of his story, I thought he must have known me, and that this was no chance encounter, he dipped his head oblivious to this dark imitating entity. He turned back to open the door, this time the entity with its white and featureless face, gazed directly at me. It dipped its head side to side like an inquisitive dog and with that they left the chapel, the sickly sour scent I thought I'd forgotten soon faded but not before I realised it was the smell of death."

"Could it have been a trick of the light Father?"

"The only trick was, no one else could see it and if they could, they did a very convincing job of not showing it."

I could see Father Martin was full of questions, the baffled look on his face prompted me to gently shake my head in his direction, hoping he would remember my words earlier that morning to allow Father Ambrose to talk unencumbered, and although his encounter with whatever it was that sent chills down my spine I knew

Father Martin and myself would have to detach our rational minds and just listen.

"So, Father, did you meet up with the gentleman at the Britannia?"

"Oh how I wish I did. By the time I arrived at the inn he had gone and all I had was this handwritten story and a journal given to me by the landlord, which completes this terrifying tale. So, I shall endeavour to tell his story as he told it to me, then and only then will you know the fear that haunts a man so close to death."

"You haven't said how you knew him Father."

"If I do not relay this story in the precious hours I have left, it will not matter how I knew him. It may seem odd for a dying man to ask patience of his audience, but I must request it."

Father Ambrose reached down to his bedside table and lifted up a leather wallet containing a large number of stained handwritten pages, the corners creased and ripped. He perched his glasses on the bridge of his nose, looked across to Father Martin, and with the sincerity of a dying man said, "If I do not see out the day Father Martin, take this manuscript and continue to read the rest without prejudice. You have the remains of the journal that I gave you yesterday?"

"I do Father, but as yet I have not read its contents."

"It serves to validate all that you will hear today. These written words sit beyond any religious philosophy you may hold dear, and I owe it to Mr Joseph Kemp to tell his extraordinary story."

His voice now soft, calm and measured, the room grew quiet, and the morning`s birdsong ceased, as if by silent behest and with this unnatural silence he lifted the first page from the wallet and began to read.

II

I may be many things, but a writer I am not, so for whomsoever reads these words in the future, take comfort that I write a story of truth, however strange and unbelievable. As a painting cannot truly convey the beauty and emotions of a rising sun, neither can the written word convince with certitude and veracity of these events. I ask no payment or patronage, but implore an open mind. The unwritten past serves only the dead, a certainty, I now, no longer fear.

Joseph Kemp – October 5th, 1919.

It's a sobering thought, but I haven't set foot in Medcott for over three decades, the place I was born all those years ago in 1867, and all that's left are disordered memories of a childhood long since passed. I really had no desire to return, if it was not for my good friend Abner

Chetwood's death, Medcott village would remain just a distant memory.

As I stand here, looking down from Valley Point, I can see nothing has really changed visually, although I don't know why I expected it to. Thirty-five years is a small passing of time, even for us mere mortals, uncomplicated and untouched by the technological advancements of the industrial revolution. Medcott's familiar cold valley air, the sweet country smell, and the light, yes, the early morning light, the unlit streets awaken with the sun's unrivalled warm glow, unlike the electric avenues and unnatural fog filled foulness of London's West End which I left several hours ago. The exchange of filth for fresh clear air was welcoming, a reminder and affirmation that I was home.

Medcott was, and is, a small village with a meagre population of farm workers, quarry men and their families. Standing high on Blackthorn Hill is an 11th century convent, home to a closed order of Basilian nuns. The sisters of St Agnes were of a strict monastic order, which kept them from village life, their days spent reciting prayer, contemplative thought, and tending their gardens for self-sufficiency. From time to time however they would assist in childbirth, if a mother presented at their door, in pain, alone and struggling. Children were considered a blessing from God and special dispensation from the Vatican allowed entry to Christian women for the sole purpose of bringing children into the world.

No one was quite sure how many sisters there were, their devout order kept the outside world at bay, but simple village life had a way of creating the most divine and the most unnerving stories of the convent and its prayerful occupants. They were in effect invisible to the advancing world, its wars, disease and poverty. No one ever saw the nuns face to face, entry was through a series of locked inner chambers, so that no exposure to the outside world would compromise the order. Even mothers that gave birth within the walls of the convent could not recall the faces or the voices of the sisters during their labour, additional supplies and support would be given once a year by the bishop during solemnity.

Of all my childhood memories, a dreadful one persists, and in my advancing years it has become more vivid and more real. As young boys me and my closest friends, Abner Chetwood and Joel Adams had a sort of mission to get a glimpse of the inside of the convent or at the very least one of the sisters. My mother would tell the story of the night I was born, if we pestered her enough.

She'd always start the story the same way.

"It was muggy and the hour was late. I knew you were coming Joseph, you were so lively that day, I could see and feel the tips of your fingers pushing me from inside, I tried to wake your father, but he was unwell with a fever."

I've since found out my father had been drinking, one of his favourite pastimes.

"So, I threw on my old coat and some boots, the oil lamp was bright enough to walk the woodland path if I went slowly. As the pain grew stronger, I feared I wouldn't make it, the trees looked like ghostly figures in the flickering light of the oil lamp. I could see shimmering misty white lights in the darkness, like dancing angels." Mother always referred to the convent as the house of angels. "They gave me the strength to carry on. I eventually reached the first of the wide stone steps up to the convent of St Agnes. I climbed for what seemed an eternity, but I had to stop and lay down, the pain was so intense. I was ready to give up, I felt a strange presence near me, just like when someone stands over you. I looked up, and called out, please help, please help me. As I lifted my head higher, I could see the shape of a twisted figure standing amongst the sharp blackthorn bushes, trapped by its barbarous thorns. It stared at the convent walls, as if it were waiting for something."

Every time mother got to that part of the story I would ask, "Weren't you scared?"

She would always reply, "I know it meant me no harm, Joseph. I managed to get to my feet and few moments later there in front of me was the arched wooden door of the convent, I knocked and knocked until a small window in the door opened, no words were spoken, a few moments later the door slowly opened. I was helped up by two small darkly clothed figures. They guided me from one room to another, large doors slammed shut behind me as the cold damp air hit me from another door opening ahead. It felt like I was there for hours. All I remember, boys, is the silent darkness, broken only by the needful and pitiful cries of what sounded like newborn babies. I could swear I heard them crying throughout my labour, but when you arrived your little cries were all I could hear and everything else disappeared into the night. The dark was disturbed only by the brief flicker of candlelight. I could not see the sisters. I felt cold hands, and an atmosphere so heavy with sorrow that I cannot fully describe. When you had been delivered, I called out several times, can I hold my baby, please can I hold my baby! It seemed such a long time before I had you in my arms, my eyes were constantly adjusting to the dim light, the shadows danced around the walls, faint faceless figures and brief flashes of white from their habits, as they gently moved within the darkness."

We would sit so quietly, listening to her every word, every now and then Joel would make a sudden move, his way of saying, I'm not scared.

"Then I remember waking up in bed, back in the cottage, your father standing over us, his eyes full of tears. I have questioned myself many times that it was all a dream but others have had the same sort of experience."

That story in all its forms has fervently remained with me, in dreams and nightmares, it always ends the same, with me being buried alive, powerless to stop the falling earth covering my paralysed body. It seemed odd, and never made much sense, that the story of my birth conjures up nightmares of my death.

Another oddity that never seemed strange back then was that Abner and Joel were also born on the same night as me, September 16th, 1867. Abner's mother, Ellie Chetwood, a nervous woman who hardly spoke a word, and her husband Cyril, a simple and humble man with no real passion for anything other than work and an ale with his friends. That same night of my birth he had helped his wife Ellie to the convent and left her at the entrance. She had told my mother that her labour was long and drawn out, so they may have shared the same experience within the walls of the convent and entered within minutes of each other.

Now, Joel's mother, Mrs Maddy Adams, was the total opposite, along with her husband Willard. Mrs Adams was confident and by all accounts a very handsome woman, she also gave birth in the early hours of the 16th, at home and with a little help from a woman called Elspeth Tanner. Elspeth had been the schoolhouse nurse for some years. Her father, George Tanner, was quite a well to do gent, who owned the village coach-house and inn. He had sent the young innocent Elspeth away to London to be trained as a nurse back in 1850, but the woman that returned was damaged by what she had seen. She served as a nurse volunteer during the Crimean War, and having witnessed so much horror and bloodshed, could no longer apply her skills to anything more than a grazed knee in the school playground, or a case of head lice.

She took great joy in new life and childbirth and with this became Medcott's self-designated midwife. Her network of mothers and their offspring in school kept her up to date with the progress of expectant mothers. She would call in frequently when childbirth was imminent, the doctor's house and hospital were at least a half day carriage ride away. Elspeth Tanner could be the difference between life and death, an asset that very few outlying villages could boast.

Although Elspeth could not abide the failings of foolish men and those that would fight, excusing their drunken brawls as an honourable challenge, the war showed her how even the most intelligent men used their fists as the ultimate weapon of choice. And so she would do the bare minimum for these men, mainly workers from the quarry that saw fit to drink every evening at her father's inn, and then argue and fight late at night below her room at the coach-house. If our fathers were involved, she would make no mistake in telling the whole class the following day how she had dressed the wounds of so and so's father and would in her own astute way shame us for having idiots for fathers, and in some way deter us kids from fighting ourselves.

So, it was obvious to all that her services were invaluable, and especially on the night Joel was born, as Maddy's husband, Willard Adams was suffering the same drink induced sleep as my useless father, George Kemp.

All three of us lived within ten minutes of each other. I think our shared birthdays, and the fact we had completely different characters, had created a bond. We acted more like brothers, we'd argue, fight, laugh, and explore Medcott and its surrounding countryside without a care in the world.

Medcott's one claim to fame was its chalk quarry, and quicklime works, a supplier to the building industry during Queen Victoria's reign, now a disused open blot on the landscape due to over mining of the chalk face. As the chalk quarry became more productive, the population grew, as did the village, the makeshift school in the old wooden village hall was replaced by a brick-built schoolhouse. Miss Watson was the only teacher, a very stern woman and a devout Catholic. If nothing else we were destined to learn how to read and write, even at its busiest there were only thirty or so pupils. School started very early and ended early, and once our chores were done, we were free to roam the hills and woods around Medcott.

The quarry was strictly off limits, firstly, all our fathers worked there apart from Joel's and it was unsafe and unstable, the two-hundred-foot chalk rock face had taken many lives, a fate that was destined for my father years later.

Other than the new brick-built school, there were only two other buildings that stood out on Medcott's ancient skyline, St Leopold's church, and the convent, the latter, which overlooked the village in its hilltop position, never really felt part of the village, then or now, and always seemed pristinely abandoned, and this is where my story really begins.

III

It was on our joint thirteenth birthdays, late summer of 1880, that we saw a nun for the very first time. We were high up on Blackthorn Hill, a wooded copse that sat below the convent. The copse was steep, the base of its slope a thick outcrop of spiney blackthorn, which then gave way to gnarled looking yew trees that defied the treacherous chalky slopes by growing anything but straight.

The dark cloaked figure appeared from nowhere. We quietly followed from afar, so she would not see us. As far as we were concerned, this was the first ever sighting of a nun from the convent. She never once turned around, but we all felt as if she was leading us somewhere. As we passed through and behind the twisted trees we lost sight of her, our path was blocked by a large, upturned tree stump. We climbed the base and peered over and there she was, static, standing on an old wooden cross laying on the ground, small flames rose from the earth as she pointed to a spot in the dirt. We all froze.

"Shit, she's seen us!"

"Pipe down Joel."

Slowly she turned to face us, but something weirdly and inexplicably pushed our heads away, almost in unison so that we would not see her face, then we all heard the words. "Mother`s waiting." As soon as the echoey voice disappeared we felt a release, and she was gone, not gone, walked away, gone disappeared.

Joel was the first to speak. "Jesus, what does that mean, you heard it, right?"

"We don't tell anyone, got it? I mean it, not a bloody word!"

Joel was quite outspoken and unpredictable, our weakest link. In all our childhood antics, if trouble was to follow, it would be down to Joel, always the first to swear, fight and lie, his father's only contribution to Joel's upbringing. Abner and myself knew all too well if anyone were to blab, it would be Joel, but we never did speak of that day again. I was the only one who saw her on one other occasion, in the same place but from a distance, and I had no urge to follow this time. Our mission to see inside the convent had been contaminated with real fear, although none of us would admit to it.

Those long days of summer in our small village of Medcott kept us out all day. Once our chores were finished, we'd take some small rations of dried biscuits, if we got thirsty we would just drink from the brook, and, if Abner never lost his nerve, we could come away with a pound or two of juicy pears from the rectory orchard, but if caught, you would never know that the reverend Rogers was a man of the cloth. He walked with the aid of a shepherd- like crook and if swung in your direction your feet would leave the ground and your backside would meet his boot on the way down. A fair price to pay if we were caught, as he never took our bounty of pears off us.

The life we had back then was simple, the whole village moved at an apathetic pace. Medcott was the total opposite of the big towns and cities that thrived on change.

Two years later in the summer of 1882 the great smallpox epidemic had spread from London and other cities to the smaller towns and villages, Medcott was no exception. All the healthy young and unmarried were sent away to live with relatives in neighbouring villages that were untouched by the disease, those with no extended families ended up in the workhouse, a prison like existence, appalling working conditions, merciless treatment, and an empty promise of safe return when the pox had gone. This was to be my fate and that of Joel's.

Our mothers had cared for the sick, until they both succumbed to smallpox themselves, many died that year. My father survived, only to be later killed in a quarry accident, Joel's father, Willard Adams, was a jack of all trades, and would lend his hand to anything for money. That included the women of the village, a tall and very distinctive man, gypsy -like in appearance, he was always seen sporting a bright red waistcoat, cravat, frock coat and a pair of very well- worn riding boots, his unkempt long black hair was the only give away that he was no gentleman. He walked with the confident swagger of a mounted officer or a squire of the manor. My father drank with him, but never trusted him.

"Lock it up, or Willard will knock it up," my father would say, not that my father worried.

Willard only had eyes for young single women. Maddy, his wife, was stylish, a live wire once and a city girl that had been tamed by the back of his hand, and trapped in Medcott by childbirth. When their son Joel was born, Willard slipped back into his libertine ways, his new son Joel, had stolen Maddy's affections, and as a mother she would no longer put up with Willard's carnal recklessness, and kicked him out. He built a small lodge on common ground to the west of the village, the only flat part of Blackthorn Hill. He continued to exchange his skills for money and drink, he took off soon after Maddy died from the pox, and having no real love for his son Joel, left him to fend for himself.

It's incomprehensible to think within two years of our thirteenth birthdays Joel and myself were in London, and in effect, orphans. We arrived to the harshness of workhouse life, disciplined, hard and ruthless. You had to keep your head down, do your work and try and keep clean in amongst the filth. I worked hard and managed to master the needle and yarn and made a name for myself; I was good with my hands, mainly leather and fabric repairs. It was a bound tailor's apprenticeship that saw my eventual release, a trade in which I have since prospered all my adult life. So I never envisioned being back here in Medcott thirty five years later, and even stranger to some, I never returned for my parent's funerals, all those years ago, workhouse law would not permit it.

My mother was one of the first to catch smallpox and die. She worked long hours washing bedding and clothing, mainly for the coach house, all those dirty sheets probably rife with the disease. Like many she was buried in a mass grave outside the village, ironically under a blanket of the Medcott quicklime. Its use had changed, from building material to burying the dead.

My father with all his faults had not signed important Poor Law Commission paperwork which would have allowed my return home after the outbreak, which ended five months later in December 1882. My father could neither read nor write, and his death, not at the hands of smallpox, but at the quarry, left me homeless. They assumed he didn't want me, and that I was at risk of absconding.

My forced departure from Medcott at fifteen years old was under a shroud of death, and now death sees me return, in the form of a telegram I received three days ago. It was sent from Cotting Telegraph House, from whom is a mystery, the message simply read: Abner. J. Chetwood, funeral of, Thursday October 2nd, 1919, at St Leopold's-Medcott-3.15 pm, please, please attend.

As for Joel, he escaped many times during his six years from St George's workhouse in Hanover Square. He was only a few miles from me at the Strand poorhouse, they eventually gave up looking for him, and he just replaced one institution for another, that being Newgate prison. It was a desperate place, populated with London's most despicable villains. We did, however, meet many times over the past thirty years, in-between his incarcerations, the bond throughout our early life, kept us connected, although inconsistent.

I had managed to reconnect with Abner as well, years after mine and Joel's unfortunate departure from Medcott. Abner was lucky enough to have an aunt, Miss Millicent Shaw, although she insisted, we call her Milly. She was Abner's mother's older sister who lived three miles or so from the village, a small secluded cottage, below Valley Point, a wooded hollow untouched by society due to its location, and the ideal place for Abner to stay until the deathly grip of smallpox had passed.

His mother Ellie and his Aunt Milly were both born in the cottage, ten years apart, they both grew up in the hollow. Ellie married Cyril Chetwood when she was very young and then moved into the village, Milly being the eldest stayed on at the cottage. Complications during Ellie's birth left the girls without a mother. Milly continued to look after her father and help in the orchards until he died twelve years later, she remained a spinster, and never really left the village. Smallpox gave her something she could never have and the comfort of keeping her sister's boy safe was a blessing for all. Abner's mother Ellie had survived the smallpox, but seeing so much death had changed her.

After Abner went to live with Milly his mother Ellie would be seen having agitated arguments with unseen people, his father Cyril had no choice but to seek help. Ellie was eventually admitted to an asylum, diagnosed with mental deterioration, Cyril was left distraught, he had lost the will to carry on. His lack of concentration and negligence when working the chalk face caused the death of three quarrymen, one being my father. His mental state after these events left him an empty shell and without a thought for Abner he took his own life.

Abner continued to live with his Aunt Milly after his father's suicide, and worked the smallholding, tending to the animals and the apple orchards, Aunt Milly's main source of income.

He eventually left when he was twenty-four, and tracked me down in London. He had been witness to Medcott's anguish and pain, but even with the story of his poor mother and father and the catalyst that saw my own father's death, he was spared the misery of London's workhouses.

After my seven-year tailoring apprenticeship I managed to secure a long lease on a basement workshop in Burlington Street, not one of London's fanciest streets, but cheap. Abner slept on the floor of my modest basement workshop for about a year, until he secured a post as a junior clerk, at an accountant's office in Threadneedle Street, after that he acquired his own lodgings. We lost touch what with work, but we tried to meet at least once a year on our birthdays. The last time we met up was just over a year ago, September 16th, 1918, our joint 51st birthday.

Joel did manage to make it on several occasions, the last being just before his fourth court appearance for street robbery, but that was ten years ago in 1908, so he may be out now. He was like a magnet for trouble, so I wasn't counting on him being here for the funeral.

I had planned on a few days in Medcott, the 2nd was a Thursday, the day of Abner's funeral. I closed up my basement shop on the Tuesday, it was a small place hidden near the bottom end of new Burlington Street, just off the overpriced Saville Row. Above me was Brooks, a milliners shop. Henry Brooks was also my landlord, he kept the rent low and we both looked after each other's shops when either was out of town. He was a stout man, and one of the most honest, he had only increased my rent once in the 28 years of my occupancy. It was little more than an oversized cellar, with pavement skylights, but it served me well.

Medcott was a two-hour ride on my trusty model H roadsters motorcycle. I left London around 3 am on Wednesday, the extra day in Medcott would be used for some sort of closure, and I was hoping that Joel would be there too. The plan was to ride down to Valley Point and arrive early morning, motorcycle willing.

Work had been good recently, and the war years saw me making and altering many officer's dress uniforms. With a military contract in place, I had good connections that kept me from the Somme and saw me working flat out assembling trench coats for Burberry. The fabric was pre-cut, so just my skill as a machinist was required, and with my new found contacts I managed to acquire as part payment, an ex-military Triumph Model H Roadster motorcycle; one of the few things that returned from the Great War unscathed, a temperamental starter, but otherwise very reliable.

London in the early hours is a very quiet place, leafy trees and stubble filled fields replaced the streetlights, fog and grandiose of London's skyline, the silhouetted trees and unsullied darkness of the countryside sent a strange shiver through me, as if Medcott was awaiting my return. It felt as if I was being summoned, and before I knew it the sun was rising over the gently rolling valleys of the downs, and I found myself passing the wide God Cake junction into Medcott village.

I had almost two days to fill before the funeral and planned on staying at the Quarry Inn if it still had rooms, but first I was to ride up to Valley Point and then down into the hollow, to see Abner's Aunt Milly, the only person who would have my address in London. She would have been well into her ninetieth year by now, and no one else could have sent the telegram. I was not sure what to expect, firstly because the telegram was sent from Cotting Telegraph House, which was twenty or so miles from Valley Point, and secondly the telegram was unsigned.

IV

∽

I had been to Aunt Milly's on many occasions, when we were kids, Abner would spend all summer with her. After our chores were done, Joel and I would head up to Valley Point, it was the highest spot looking west across to Medcott. A large but flat moss covered stone lay along the edge of the ridge, and a tall upright stone stood to its left, hence the name Valley Point, it was like a warning stone, as beyond that was a sheer drop into the valley below. When we were young, we dared each other to see who could sit nearest the edge, we'd sing out loud, "Go on, go on, go on Joel, closer, get closer you chicken."

Joel was always the winner; Abner and I would just end up throwing stones into the valley below. A well-worn track led down into the valley and continued into the village three miles away. Aunt Milly was like everyone's mother, and insisted "just call me Milly." She never married but would have loved to have had children.

I recognised the cottage as soon as I saw it in the distance, you could still make out the crudely painted name on the stone wall, Hollow Oak Cottage. There was a wide and deep stream that ran so close to the cottage it always looked as if it were sinking into the dark waters. The cottage was pristine, with a beautiful climbing wisteria covering the walls and an abundance of rose bushes, strangely still in bloom this late in the year.

I cut the engine and let the bike coast down to the gate, so as not to startle the old girl. The model H Roadster's engine was like an excited tractor and quite often mis-fired when dropping the revs, but Aunt Milly was already standing there in the porch, as if I had knocked seconds earlier. I stood the bike up on its stand and walked over.

"You've not changed a bit little Joseph."

She'd not seen me in thirty-five years, so I guessed her eyes were not so good.

"Come in and let me have a proper look at you."

We sat and had tea, and talked about Abner for what seemed like hours. I had to ask the question.

"Do you know how it happened? Your telegram was very short."

She looked at me with a vacant expression, she explained that she had not sent any telegram.

"But how did you know I would be coming?" I asked.

"The only people that comes to see me Joseph, is Father Daniels, and old nosey Elspeth, she brings me a weekly food hamper and my mail and the occasional newspaper, and when she brought me this sad letter, I knew you would follow soon. Abner spoke of you many times on his visits to see me, he said he always felt a connection with you, and that wayward boy Joel. He wanted to repay your generosity because of your help when he was finding his way in London, he said you would always see him right." She lay the letter down on the table. "It's from Abner's employer, fancy paper, with an embossed letterhead, all nicely written, please read it Joseph, but not out loud."

September 30th, 1919

Dear Miss Millicent Shaw,

It is a matter of sincere regret that I have to inform you of the death of Abner James Chetwood, he was a very valued member of our accounts firm for nearly thirty years.

Our employee records show that you are his next of kin, and also his benefactor if anything untoward were to happen, and as his only blood relative we will graciously take instruction from you as to the repatriation of his body back to Medcott. It would be a privilege for Cranbrook and Cranbrook to cover all costs for Abner's funeral and any other monies required for his coffin and pallbearers. His unfortunate demise was on company time and although not linked to his work its circumstances are baffling to me, James, and my brother, Albert Cranbrook, who mentored Abner in his early years with the company.

I enclose a cheque payable as cash of £36 pounds and 4 shillings, Abner's final pay and commission to the year end. I am obliged to enclose herewith the police report, from Whitechapel police station, from the acting officer on duty for the 16th of September 1919.

I hope the report below does not cause you too much distress, if there was any way of sparing you this dreadful information I would, but Whitehall government protocol dictates that the police evidence and coroner's verdict be passed on to the next of kin.

With regards and deepest sympathy

James Cranbrook Esq.

Police report – September 16th, 1919 – Leman Street Police Station, Whitechapel, London. Detective Constable Howard attending and Constable Bartholomew.

On the night of September 16th, 1919, whilst on business for Cranbrook's Accountants, Abner James Chetwood Esq jumped naked from the fourth-floor bedroom window of the Gunthorpe Street hotel in Whitechapel, London. Tied to his wrist was a small tailor's price tag with the address of Kemps tailors, Burlington Street, London. He had neatly folded his suit, shirt, tie, and laid them out on his bed.

The investigating officer, Detective Constable Howard, is satisfied that there was no evidence of foul play. The reverse of the tailor's price tag attached to his wrist, had the words "Mother's waiting" written upon it, this has been filed as evidence and the incident has been recorded by the second attending police officer, Constable Bartholomew, and in his report, written under the supervision of Detective Howard, has been recorded as death by misadventure. The investigating officer has therefore concluded that suicide is the most likely cause but with the absence of no actual suicide note, and only one eyewitness, who reported seeing a woman of small stature wearing dark clothing tending to Mr Chetwood soon after the incident, we believe that said person may have left the scene in a state of shock having witnessed the fall and the extent of Mr Chetwood's injuries, we see no connection or reason for further investigation, therefore the coroner's final verdict is death by suicide and cause of death fatal head trauma.

I folded the letter and placed it on the table, Aunt Milly picked it up and placed it in her pinny pocket. Joel, Abner and I had never spoken a word to anyone in the village, about the nun, or "Mother's waiting" it was all too crazy, and for fear of being laughed at, we never even discussed it amongst ourselves. We all saw and heard it without any doubt, all those years ago and if it wasn't for those two words now written on one of my tailor's price tags I could have just said goodbye to Abner on Thursday, and left Medcott as quickly as I arrived.

I looked across at Aunt Milly, a tear slowly ran down her gently creased cheek, she stared right through me, as if I wasn't there, the hairs on the back of my neck rose and a cold shiver ran down my spine, there was a loud knock at the door. I jumped up quick.

"I'll get it."

Any excuse to break Aunt Milly's cold distant gaze, there came a second knock, much louder this time, followed by a deep voice.

"Is anyone there?"

As I neared the door, I could see a pile of old newspapers and some letters, wedged underneath.

I responded, "Yes, give me a minute."

I pulled the papers out of the way and went to grab the handle, but that was also on the floor, how did I not notice this when I entered?

"Hang on!" I shouted.

I lifted the letterbox flap, slipped my hand through and pulled the door open. There, standing in the doorway was a tall man, large black broad-brimmed hat, long coat and white collar, I assumed it was Father Daniels.

"Can I help you son?"

"One minute Father." I turned and gently shouted back toward the living room. "It's the father, Aunt Milly."

There was no response, I turned back, held out my hand. "Joseph Kemp, pleased to meet you Father."

"Likewise, I'm Father Daniels, I look in every now and then, to check on the cottage."

I turned and walked back to the living room, the hairs on my neck once again stood on end, the mirror in the hallway along with the mismatched paintings were covered in cobwebs and dust.

"Can I help you with something Joseph?"

I started to explain I was here for the funeral of Abner Chetwood. Father Daniels followed me into the living room, and went over to the window and drew back the curtains, unlatched the windows and pushed them open.

"Sad business Joseph, you knew him well?"

I replied that I did, like a brother, sort of. The room was suddenly filled with shards of light, visible as the dust hung on the thin rays piercing the room, there where I had sat just minutes earlier, drinking tea and eating cake, was now a dusty table, the teapot, cups and cake covered with the mould and detritus of human absence.

"What troubles you Joseph?"

My confusion and fear were apparent. Could I even try and explain that I'd just been talking to Aunt Milly for what seemed like hours, the now uninhabited cottage, the absence of Aunt Milly. I tried to explain, albeit not very convincingly. I'd never believed in a God or anything spiritual. Father Daniel's answer was of no comfort.

"When we need answers Joseph, we connect with what memories we have left, to create a place that feels like home, some questions have no answer. Millicent, Miss Shaw, died almost a year ago, it was around this time, late September. I promised to keep an eye on the place until Mr Chetwood had time to fix it up and let the cottage out, but sadly, that won't happen now."

I grabbed my jacket and headed out to my bike, Father Daniels followed close by, pulling the door shut behind him, he walked off down toward the valley path and without turning round, lifted his hat.

"I'll close the windows on my return, give it a good airing, we'll see you Thursday Joseph, I have a few things for you to sign and maybe we can discuss things further if you're still feeling confused."

I rolled the bike down to the woodshed, Triumph Roadsters had an awful turning circle, and the path was much wider there. I turned and pushed the bike back up toward the cottage, the wisteria was now mangled and overgrown, reaching up and into the upstairs windows, entwined through the small square metal frames where the glass panes once sat. The beautiful rose bushes, now ugly, flowerless brambles that had become one with the old painted garden fence and there in the living room, sitting in the window, was Aunt Milly, a small dark figure stood to her left, a nun-like habit obscured all but its mouth. It barked a frenzy of silent words into Aunt Milly's ear, its shoulders contorted, blackened teeth glistened with a viscous saliva, it was manic, like a mad dog restrained by a short leash. Milly's gaze, once again, looking at and right through me, her eyes locked beyond me, and beyond life.

I had seen many a thing I could not explain, life, death and everything in-between, all those years ago in the workhouse, but never had my ghosts been so real. I reached down to the bike's starter handle. I cranked the engine into life.

I'd only taken my eyes off the cottage for a few seconds. Aunt Milly's spectre, or whatever it was, was unnerving enough, but the thrashing mouth of that muted soul was inhuman. I looked up with fearful anticipation, what would be next? To my relief the window was empty, and all that remained was nature's reclamation of Aunt Milly's cottage. I kept the revs high and raced the bike up to the road, my mind numb with trepidation. Was this unearthly encounter the end or the beginning of my lamentable return?

I rode with great haste down to the God Cake junction, right, into Medcott or left for Cotting? I needed to secure my lodgings, so Medcott it was.

The Quarry Inn was on the edge of the village. I pulled into the wide empty courtyard; to say it was run down would be an understatement. It was originally called Tanner's Coach House; the original sign still hung over the archway to the coach shed and stables. Expansion of the quarry works years back saw it renamed, partly due to the influx of more quarrymen working at the chalk face. At shift end, the place would come to life, cheap ale and basic grub, this was to the dismay of many a wife and mother.

It appeared to be closed, curtains drawn and no sign of life anywhere. I knocked a few times, an upstairs window opened, a fat faced gent leaned out.

"We're closed chum."

I shouted up. "I just need some lodgings, two nights."

The window slammed shut, and a few minutes later a rotund red-faced man opened the door.

"It's one crown per night, in advance, evening meal and a glass of ale included and you'll have to move that thing round back, if you value it, that is."

"I'm sure no one's going to steal it?"

He laughed. "Steal it? My clientele don't know their arse from their elbows, and trust me after six or seven jars, their motor cars and your bike will become acquainted, they'll be gone and your ten shillings will increase whilst you get it fixed, if you can get it fixed."

I unhooked my side bags from the bike, the landlord led me through to the back of the inn, and up to a small room.

"Here you go, hot water's on at four, food at six, mind the low beam and the loose floorboard by the window, if you need owt else, you'll have to get it from Cotting, that'll be ten shillings."

I unpacked my clothes and laid my suit out on the bed; a few days should see the creases settle, the ride and morning's events had left me quite drained, but I had no intention of resting, especially as the room was cramped. There was a wooden chair near the window and a heavily stained basin and jug on a washstand in the corner, I had the feeling the cheery fat-faced landlord had not changed the bedding since its last occupants. Its only saving grace was the view, a small glimpse of the bright weathered stonework of the convent and the imposing steep elevation of Blackthorn Hill. The vast woods surrounding the convent had matured in my absence, shielding some of its grandeur, but between the tall yew trees, the belfry was unmistakable.

It was a quarter past eleven, so I headed down to the inn, which was situated at the front of the building. It looked out onto the main road through Medcott, half a dozen mismatched tables, an uneven floor and small inglenook fireplace, it was deserted, apart from the landlord, who was mumbling to himself behind the bar. He looked up, knocked back a glass of something.

"If you want ale, we open at twelve."

"No", I replied, he then continued mumbling to himself. "Do you know where I can get some fuel?"

"As I said, chum, everything's in Cotting."

His hospitality was about as welcoming as his pokey room, but I had to ask the burning question.

"Is anyone else staying here for the funeral on Thursday?"

Being a small village, everyone knew everyone's business.

"I don't know chum, I don't ask folk why they stay here."

I thought to myself, maybe you should, it certainly wasn't for the warm conversation.

V

⌒⌒⌒

I headed out to Cotting, fuel was essential and some food. It was a market town that I never had much exposure to as a boy. It was good day's walk to the outskirts from Medcott village, around eighteen miles or so, even as energetic boys we couldn't do that in a day. I had enough fuel to get there and a bit spare, so I rode through the village and turned around in the school courtyard; it looked the same, like the inn, a bit run down, out front was a coach stop sign, a bench, and a large painted advertising board, the Westbrook Coach Company. In the 1880's it was either horse and cart or walk.

Seeing the village early this morning from Valley Point, before the events at Aunt Milly's, had left me feeling a sense of immense nostalgia. I'd come home, and for a few moments it felt like I had stepped back to when I left, shattered by the revenant Aunt Milly and her spectre, combined with the happy landlord and now a bus route out of Medcott. The place had changed, and I realised my nostalgia was just a subconscious memento that no longer existed, there was truly nothing here, but the ghosts of my past and Abner's funeral would close the chapter of a long overdue homecoming.

The Triumph made light work of the ride into Cotting. I fuelled up on the edge of town, at Baxter's service station, and managed to get some bread and a half-pound of cheese, even though it was well after twelve pm, another reminder of the backward pace of country life. In London I'd usually buy a small hob loaf from Turners in Regents Street, but you could forget it after nine am, they'd sell out, due to supplying all the local hotels.

Second stop was Telegraph House, where my telegram originated. The office looked empty, but I could hear the clicking sound of a telegraph machine. I went over to the counter.

"Good morning, sir."

"Morning, I was wondering if you could help me?" I passed the telegram through the slot to the clerk. "Is there any way of finding out who sent this?"

The operator glanced at the telegram. "It has a sender code on the back sir."

"It does?" I answered.

"R Ft, Fellows, right there in that box sir."

"Any idea who that is and where I might find them?"

"Reverend Father Fellows sir, either at the church, on Oswald's Road, Mass finished around nine, so the rectory would be your best bet sir, are you from out of town?"

"Yes."

"Which way did you come in from?"

"Medcott."

"On the bus?"

"No, motorcycle."

"If you head back the way you came, for about six miles, and look out for a right-hand turn just past the milestone, it's a narrow track, fairly well hidden. It's the only house down there, you can't miss it."

I tried the church first, but it was all locked up, the notice board informed me that Mass was at eight am and five pm on Wednesdays, so I left Cotting for the rectory. It was now around two pm, and I wanted to at least get some closure on the telegram, as I had no recollection of a Reverend Fellows.

The track was indeed very narrow, and heavily rutted, enough room for a small motor car, but very bumpy. I arrived at the house, it was large and quite imposing, very gothic in appearance, almost ugly. Surrounded by tall, dark, evergreen trees, it was a creepy place and as far from anything holy as I could imagine.

As I cut the engine, I had a moment of Deja vu. The Reverend was standing in the large porch and appeared to be waiting for me. Flashbacks of Aunt Milly this morning pulsed through my head, my hands sweating, a rush of adrenaline surged through my body to start the engine and leave.

"Good afternoon."

Too late, he started to walk over, I calmed myself. He looked real, but then so did Aunt Milly.

"How can I help you?"

"Good afternoon, Reverend."

"Father Fellows, please."

"My name is Joseph Kemp, I used to live in Medcott many years ago. I have returned for my friend`s funeral, Abner Chetwood."

"Oh yes, unfortunate business, did you say Joseph?"

"Yes, I received an unsigned telegram a few days back, I've just left the telegraph operator in Cotting. He explained how to identify the sender, and gave me directions to the rectory."

"Come, come inside Joseph, we have much to discuss."

So far, so good. As we entered, I made a mental memory of the inside, unlike Aunt Milly's, this place was already in a run-down state.

The Father led me through to the kitchen, he called out, "Mrs Cooper, Mrs Cooper."

A small elderly woman shuffled into the room, she spoke with a strong Irish accent. "Yes, your holiness."

"Can you make some tea Mrs Cooper and bring it through to the study?"

"Yes, your holiness."

I had to bite my lip. Each time she spoke she would dip her head a small amount, as if Father Fellows was the pope, it was the first bit of hilarity I had experienced all day. We walked through to the study.

"Please, take a seat Joseph."

We sat facing each other, separated by a large wooden desk with fancy leather inlays. Father Fellows proceeded to fumble through a large set of keys attached to an even larger silver ring.

"Got it. So many keys, so few secrets."

He unlocked the top drawer on his side of the desk, and drew out a brown leather messenger bag, then laid the contents out in front of me.

"There is a mix of correspondences here Joseph, some you might find relevant and a few pieces of mail delivered to the house after Miss Shaw's passing."

My eye was instantly drawn to the red wax seal and letter from Cranbrook and Cranbrook, addressed to Miss Shaw. It was open and appeared to have been read, further throwing my sensibility into question.

Mrs Cooper entered with the tea, set the tray down on the corner of the desk, and poured out two cups.

"Please help yourself to milk and sugar, will there be anything else your holiness?"

"No Mrs Cooper."

She dipped her head and left.

"I know, Joseph. She's been with me for a long time and has never called me by my ordained name, which can make for very awkward conversations when the bishop visits, as not even he is addressed with such grandeur. So, Joseph, you'll be wanting some answers. Firstly I did send the telegram, this was under the instruction of Miss Shaw down in Valley Point. She had sent me a letter over a year ago, and some other written documents, her original letter is amongst this lot somewhere. As you probably know Mr Chetwood, Abner, visited his aunt two or three times a year, she contacted me as her health was failing, and she had concerns for Abner's well-being; he refused to seek help from friends or any medical advice or intervention, he feared ending up like his poor mother Mrs Chetwood. I assume you know the history?"

"I know she was admitted to an asylum over thirty years ago. He did visit when he could, but never discussed the place, and he never said that he needed help."

"Miss Shaw asked me to send you a telegram if anything untoward happened to Abner, she supplied me with your London address. I did visit her to discuss the matter in great detail, regarding Abner's worrying letter, which you can read later at your leisure. Before I left that afternoon, she made me swear on the bible, that I would only contact you in the event of some tragedy, but made it very clear that her death was not such an occasion."

"How did she die Father?"

"Two days after my visit, her friend Miss Elspeth Tanner was delivering some flour and provisions, she had a key so let herself in. Miss Tanner is a very spritely lady for her advanced years and regularly walks the three miles with great haste to the Hollow. She went through to the kitchen and put away the provisions and then proceeded to clean up, chatting away to Miss Shaw in the front room, it was only when she entered, that she realised Miss Shaw was dead. It was a great shock to her. She was sat in her old chair staring out of the window, eyes wide open, as if she was still alive, clutching, no gripping, an old journal for dear life. She believed it to be a prayer book and thought Miss Shaw had taken some comfort in its words, knowing her end was imminent, it's here amongst the letters somewhere."

"Did Abner attend the funeral Father?"

"He did but left soon after, however he met with Father Daniels, the parish priest. He supplied him with the deeds to the cottage and instruction on its upkeep, you'll meet him tomorrow."

"We have already been acquainted."

"Did you see him in the village?"

I just answered yes, with no mention of the morning's bizarre and chilling events. At this point, I was anxious to gather up the paperwork and head back to my pokey room in Medcott to read Aunt Milly's letters, hoping they could explain the unexplainable.

"Father Daniels is the parish priest and deals with the day to day ecumenical concerns of the parishioners. Miss Shaw felt, due to the nature of her nephew`s letter and subsequent dilemma, that a higher clerical office might be needed. Her letter of instruction was for me to deal with this sensitive matter, so I apologise for the brevity and limited words used on the telegram. Her request to contact you was a living one, so for obvious reasons, it did not seem appropriate to sign as her, after her passing, so I hope that has cleared up that mystery. Miss Shaw has always been a devoted member of the church in Medcott; even when she could no longer walk the three miles for Sunday Mass, she would always give access to the church volunteers and the verger to pick and use her lovely blooms for the church's functions.

"According to Father Daniels, the property, garden and orchards have relinquished their beauty and fallen foul of mother nature's grasp. I think Miss Shaw was the last resident that was born and lived in Medcott all her life. So, it only seemed fitting to assist her as much as I could. I did suggest to Miss Shaw on the afternoon that we met, that a friend could possibly make sense of poor Abner's suffering, without the need for medical intervention, but she said if Abner wished to talk to anyone, he would have to do it on his own volition. She was adamant that he would accept no help. Abner had spoken to his aunt of his visits to his mother, the disturbed and seemingly uninhabited mind of

Mrs Chetwood did haunt him. I have myself visited Cane Hill Lunatic Asylum and it is a distressing place."

Father Fellows seemed nervous and was constantly moving the letters around the desk. I could now see the leather-bound book he mentioned, a solid brass plate attached to the front and back, and a key lock clasp. There appeared to be more letters inserted into its pages, visible from the book's cover.

"And the book Father?"

"That is the very same book Miss Shaw was clutching, Miss Tanner gave it to me at the funeral. I am not sure if it is a bible, prayer book or just a journal." Father Fellows fumbled through the bag. "Unfortunately, there is no key, there is also an unopened letter, which Father Daniels gave to me a few weeks after Miss Shaw's funeral. Her address is clearly marked on the back, and the post office has stamped it, return to sender, unfortunately the ink has run, and the recipient's address is unreadable."

Father Fellows stood up, gathered all the paperwork up and placed it all back, and then handed me the leather bag. We finished our tea, he then called out to Mrs Cooper.

"Don't think me rude Joseph, but I must prepare for evening Mass at five, I do hope the letters and book can answer some of the mystery around Miss Shaw's arrangements and maybe a clue into Abner's suffering. My blessing and peace go with you for Thursday. I bid you good day."

"Mrs Cooper, Mrs Cooper, see Mr Kemp out, will you."

VI

I arrived back at the inn just before four pm, with the anticipation that the promised hot water would be forthcoming, it was, and enough to rid myself of the day`s grime. I opened the messenger bag and took the letters down to the bar; the plan was to read the journal later, as it was clearly not a prayer book, but someone's treasured journal. The letters hopefully would clarify what Abner could not communicate to me this past year.

There were several letters, some, just general correspondences, with dates and times of Abner's plans to visit Aunt Milly. Cranbrook's letter, an eerie reminder of this morning`s unexplained events, and Milly's unopened return to sender. I started with Abner's two-page letter, the one Father Fellows alluded to, which had caused the concern with Aunt Milly, it reads.

Dearest Aunt Milly   *September 16th, 1918*

I have of late been feeling quite out of sorts and I may not be able to make my planned journey on the 24th of September. I am still plagued with the apparition that we discussed so many times. I did not have the courage to bring it into the conversation with Joseph this afternoon when we met for our birthday tea. I now feel a sense of guilt, having had the benefit of your guidance, and your first-hand knowledge regarding conversations with my mother before she was committed into Cane Hill Asylum. What started as just featureless shapes in the dark all those years ago when I lived with you, is now an entity that follows me and by my reckoning is very real. Whatever it is that hides in the shadows I feel it waiting, waiting for me to acknowledge its presence. I fear the dark of night and the shadows by day, my reluctance to fully accept its existence keeps me from going mad. I am very reticent to announce to anyone that I am being haunted by a figure in the darkness.

Once again, the hairs on my neck stood on end, I can now understand Aunt Milly's concern. As the letter said, we had met last year on our birthday. We had a delightful afternoon tea at the Grosvenor House Hotel, which was strange. Abner was very cautious with money, he had lost a lot of his savings ten years back to a flamboyant and tarty showgirl called Lillian who he had fallen for. They planned to marry, but Lillian and her brother had hoodwinked

Abner and left London with their travelling show and his savings. It's a long story, but he ended up with just the shirt on his back, since then he has been very frugal, to say the least. So, afternoon tea at the Grosvenor was a real extravagance.

He insisted we sat in the window looking out onto Park Lane, our normal meetups were usually late and after work, the Blind Beggar in Whitechapel a favourite haunt of ours, cheap ale and cheap food.

"What will you be having sir?"

Before I could speak, the barmaid barked, "Meat stew and potatoes or potatoes and meat stew."

It was an attempt at humour, but her face said otherwise, I don't normally make assumptions, but it was obvious this was the landlord's wife.

"You'll be having a glass of ale sir?"

Again, this was more of an order as opposed to a question, I replied "Yes please."

It's a shame Joel was not here, I almost expected him to walk into the bar, he had a very sharp wit, a real dandy. Unlike Abner, Joel was no fool when it came to women, they adored his wayward charm which he duly took advantage of, along with their purses and whatever else he could pocket before leaving their abode in the morning, but I had not seen him in many, many years, the last time we did meet he was much quieter and very polite, as if prison time had started to tame his immoral soul.

For me there was only one, my lovely Evie, we met seventeen or so years ago. She was a downstairs kitchen maid at Abervale House in Chelsea. Back then I always hand-delivered my tailored suits and shirts, also curtain and bedding repairs, it was good for business. I would enter through the back, tradesmen only, and that's where I met my Evie, seventeen years later and she's now housekeeper.

We planned to save up and, well, I don't know what really, we would talk about marriage, children and moving out of London, buy a smallholding in the country and leave the life of servitude, raise goats and chickens, but it never happened.

"Meat stew, glass of ale."

"Lovely."

It actually tasted good, the ale was a bit sharp, but welcome after a long day, I continued to read.

Not to reiterate but I must conclude that this is not the onset of madness. I have indulged my fearful curiosity with a spiritualist medium, a Miss Eleanor Carter. Our first and only meeting ending with solemn affirmation that I was in grave danger. The sitting, with its obvious fakery, left me in no doubt this thing that lay waiting in the shadows was undeniably evil. Miss Carter a convincing creator of ghosts and who's mediumship was pure deception and hoax was left emphatically convinced that her theatrical conjuring and peddling of fictitious spirits was no longer something to be trifled with. She has now ceased her service to contact the dead, a testimony to my faith and belief that this creature would forever seek to do me harm.

Before this morning's encounter at the cottage I would have pulled Abner's leg rotten, although Joel was the worst for believing the most fantastical stories, and the telling of. They were both well aware of my dismissive nature regarding anything relating to the extraordinary and supernatural, not that this explains Abner's reluctance to speak to me, the contents of this first page truly showed the fear he was suffering. I ordered another glass of ale and read on.

I will follow your advice Aunt Milly and keep myself from dwelling on what might be in the darkness, and as you mentioned, that which sealed my poor mother's fate was unseen, but yet her misery and melancholy were for all to see, a road I wish not to travel. If the intensity and frequency of this darkness increases I will contact Joseph before I confront that which only I can see. I will write and keep you informed of this matter regularly, and of my plans to visit within the next few weeks.

Kindest Regards
Abner. J. Chetwood

The letter ended there. The second page had a single paragraph on, this had been smudged whilst the ink was wet and was unreadable, similar to Aunt Milly's returned letter. Abner wrote this over a year ago, and never contacted me once about his fears.

It had been a long tiring day, the effects of the second ale had taken hold, and I felt quite high and sleepy at the same time, the rest could wait until the morning. I had most of the next day to continue with the letters and the journal. I bid the landlady good night and retired to my room.

The bed's small size and simple construction, not to mention ancient mattress and bedding would not hamper my need for sleep. I left my long-johns on, to give some buffer between the sheets and my body, the window was small and curtain-less.

The waxing moon gently illuminated the small room. I pondered over Abner's words but soon found the ale and my day's exploits weighing heavy on my eyes.

I was awoken what seemed like minutes after I had fallen asleep, the landlord was outside my door. It sounded like he was arguing, there was a bit of a scuffle, someone shouted, "Pipe down!"

They lowered their voices but continued to argue, the room was much darker now as the moonlight had diminished. The landlord had moved further down the landing. All I could hear were inaudible mumbles. I rolled over to face the window, and made myself jump. In the dim light the washstand and jug looked like a person sitting in the corner. I desperately tried to make my eyes and my brain see it as a jug and stand, but to no avail, then the tapping started, tap, tap, tap, the sound of long nails on porcelain. The curtains moved, but there were no curtains, something dressed in black was standing in the corner. I have never believed in a God, ghosts or spirits, and in one day, I have been confronted with a revenant Aunt Milly, a spectre and now having read one of Abner's letters, I fear this darkness is one and the same thing.

I turned once again to face the door. I felt a warm clammy breath on my face, it was as if someone was lying on me breathing into my ear, and then those words, I'd laid to rest a lifetime ago. "Mother`s waiting." I jumped up and struck my head on the large beam above the bed.

I awoke the next day on the floor, nursing a large bump, and an aching body. I threw on my old trousers and jacket and headed downstairs, the clock in the bar read 2.15 pm, the landlord was clearing glasses.

"Is that correct?" I asked.

"It was the last time I looked."

I had lost almost the whole day; I suspect making contact with the large oak beam and the strong ale was the cause of my lengthy sleep.

No hot water until four, so I did my best to look presentable for the funeral at a quarter after three. My suit still looked crumpled, a perfect match for the rest of my miserable appearance.

St Leopold's was only a few minutes' walk from the inn. I broke off some of yesterday's bread and a chunk of cheese, and headed down to the bar.

"Large brandy please landlord."

"Good stuff or medical grade?"

"Good stuff please."

I could just make out Father Daniels sitting in the window, drinking tea, I walked over.

"Good day Joseph, Dutch courage?"

"Sort of, Father" I replied.

Other than us the place was empty.

"I'm glad I've seen you before the service Joseph, I have something for you."

He handed me a large, folded document, of several pages, on the back a handwritten message. *"To my Dearest friend Joseph, please accept this title deed of ownership, for Hollow Oak Cottage."*

I was quite shocked, Aunt Milly's cottage, was now mine. A sudden unwanted flashback struck me, my encounter last night, the darkness, this thing of indefinite shape, it was now becoming clear that I had felt its presence before, the same fear rushed through my body.

"Sit down Joseph, you're looking quite peaky."

I sat and read on.

I have instructed Father Daniels as executor of my estate to gift Aunt Milly's cottage to yourself and Evie in the event of my death, it goes only part way to thank you for your loyal friendship, I only wished that we could have spent more of our lives together. I hope the cottage will give yourself and Evie incentive enough to follow your plans to settle in the country, your loyal friend Abner. J Chetwood.

The letter was addressed to Father Daniels and dated 15th of September 1919, the day before Abner's supposed suicide. It seemed Abner had all his final wishes in order, Cranbrooks to cover and organise his burial, and Father Daniels to tie up his estate.

I still found it hard to swallow that he stepped out of that window for fear of ending his days in an asylum. His letter to Aunt Milly made clear he was under no delusion, this entity was real. Something that I would be remiss to ignore.

Father Daniels stood up, checked his pocket watch.

"There are documents to sign Joseph, but we can do that later."

It was quite overwhelming, a whole lifetime away from Medcott and now I have the opportunity to return and start a new life where I left an old one.

"Walk with me Joseph, it's time to say goodbye to your friend."

We arrived to an empty church and Abner's casket, a dark wooden ornate box with brass handles. Four stocky men, from the undertakers, were chatting in the doorway.

"Afternoon sir. Afternoon Father."

It was peculiar and quite awkward to be the only friend saying goodbye to Abner. I had the feeling that Joel would still walk in at some point, but the reality was that Newgate's grip would probably never see him a free man.

Father Daniel's words were more connected than most, he at least knew Abner. I did consider saying a few words, but what could I say to an empty church, it would be self-serving, the only person who would have benefited is dead in a wooden box before me.

The four respectful pallbearers performing their role once more, carried Abner to his final resting place, a peaceful spot, away from the numerous lines of subsided headstones. There was a strong breeze, the sunlight dipping in and out of the clouds, and a pureness in the air that reminded me of those long summers we had all spent exploring Medcott as young lads. They lowered the coffin into the ground, Father Daniels said a few more words and then left me to say goodbye.

For the first time since hearing of Abner's death I had an overwhelming feeling of sadness, but as I walked away my mind felt free and since arriving back in Medcott I felt at ease.

I returned to the inn, my motivation to continue reading the remaining contents of the messenger bag had lost any kind of urgency. Still, I owed it to Abner to get closure, although it would change nothing.

There used to be a small park situated near the other end of the village. The evening air was clear, and with an hour or so left of warm sunlight I walked down and sat on one of the cast iron benches.

I was going to start with the journal. The secure clasp and lock indicated it was a private journal. I tried to prise the clasp open, but my penknife was back in the room, and the lock although small was very robust, so I decided to open the letter that had been returned to sender. Aunt Milly had clearly put her address on the back, and dated it September 25th 1918.

I opened the letter, the handwriting was precise and beautifully written, small drips of water had run down the page mixing with the ink to form tears of blue watercolour.

My Dearest Abner

I hope with all my heart that this letter reaches you with God speed, I cannot explain with complete certainty but must endeavour to do so and with great haste. Your life is in danger. I received your letter dated the sixteenth of September a few days ago, a day later a small leather journal with a brass locking clasp and key was left at my door. This journal has revealed in great detail some dreadful and frightening events of 1867. I cannot express my fear enough and would happily dismiss this written account, but for the fact, the author of this journal was the last serving Abbess of St Agnes's, who according to Elspeth, died in 1880. I must also inform you that since your last letter I too have been haunted by a presence that makes no attempt to hide its dark form. It stands uncomfortable close to me at night and chatters in my ear. It fades in the daylight, so I have taken to sitting in the window, as the light of day permits some solace from whatever it is, but as the light fades, I can sense its aggravation.

This journal has unlocked a long-kept secret. I cannot explain the contents, but will send it to you as soon as I finish this letter, but Abner I implore you, contact Joseph and tell him of your suffering, both of you must not return to Medcott. I believe this malevolent darkness means me no harm, of that I am sure. I can write no more, my thoughts are being tainted and seduced by its presence, it tempts me to invite you here, do not come. Abner, trust your eyes and your heart.

Aunt Milly

Now I was worried, this letter had not reached Abner, something made sure of that. Written and sent just before Aunt Milly died, a whole year ago, and whatever this journal contains that is now in my possession, I can only assume Abner like me had not read its contents either.

Poor old Aunt Milly, she had reached out to me yesterday morning from wherever her spirit was caught. I'm in no doubt as to the creature jabbering in her ear, Abner's shadow dweller and my visitor last night are one and the same thing, my scepticism would now no longer protect me. If this book held all the answers, I must accept the unimaginable and presume that both their deaths were no accident. I reached for the journal, and started to strike the clasp against the bench, with the first blow a key fell, hidden within the spine, I unlocked it and opened the journal.

VII

~~~

Two letters had been inserted into the centre of the journal, both with wax seals from the Vatican City, from a Father Gabriel Donato. I put these to one side and started to read the journal.

Deus est omniscient December 25th, 1866

I write this journal of events, as Abbess of St Agnes's, Medcott, to document and report that Sister Emeline took leave of her senses, as yet for unknown reasons and left the convent late on Christmas Day 1866. Our order has seen fit to exist in absolute confinement, and in eight hundred years of our divine servitude no sister has broken her vow of embodiment within these walls. Sister Emeline returned half-naked with her face and body bruised, distraught, repeating the name incubus, incubus.

We settled her and tended to her injuries. We had no choice but to isolate her from the other sisters and confine her to her cell. Sister Mary and I have taken it upon ourselves to nurse her broken mind and body in complete isolation of all other sisters, and until such time God alone shall be her judge and protector.

During the passing weeks she has become almost mute, and speaks only of the name incubus. Of our few monastic scholarly books we learnt that incubus is a most foul and ancient demon that lies upon and seduces sleeping women. Our prayers were many, but all attempts to free Sister Emeline from the belief that she had colluded with this obscene beast were to no avail, within a few months it was obvious that Sister Emeline was with child. In her shame she reversed her pure white wimple to cover her face. She feared no sister should see this most unholy sight.

We prayed every day in chapel, but from her room she could be heard cursing in unison, speaking in tongues and Latin, Adflixit et reddere, incubus will pay, over and over, she would repeat those vengeful words.

Word was sent to the Vatican and by the time his most holiness Pope Pius IX had given his advocate Father Gabriel Donato permission to travel the long journey from Rome Sister Emeline was near full term.

Father Donato was graced with immeasurable power, an investigator and exorcist, a communicator with things beyond our spiritual doctrine of prayer and contemplation. He was to be given access to Sister Emeline for the sole purpose of mental examination, and to free her of this evil burden. Only if he was convinced of possession and of the unholy creation within her would he perform the De exorcismis et supplicationibus quibusdam, the rite of exorcism.

His meeting took place on the morning of August twelfth, 1867, at seven am, in the outer cloister of the convent. Sister Emeline and Father Donato would be the only ones present. Two chairs were prepared, Sister Emeline continued to wear her wimple in reverse, we had no choice but to alter her gown to accommodate the unborn child, which was now unmistakable under her habit.

We passed the key through the small hatch to Father Donato on his arrival, so he could gain access, Sister Mary and myself then retired to the convent, locking the outer cloister door. It was in Father Donato's hands now. We could hear raised voices and Sister Emeline's frequent profanities, it was hours before the room fell silent, and then we heard the door to the convent slam shut. We knew Father Donato had left. Sister Emeline was weak and could hardly stand, she looked drained and for a few days seemed free of her relentless cursing.

We would have to wait a few days for Fathers Donato's report. His journey had taken weeks from Rome, by ship and stagecoach to Medcott, so a few more days to see the end of this terrible situation were seen as a blessing. He was given lodging at Tanner's Coach-House, and would return his findings as soon as he could, his meticulously typed report was hand delivered a few days later.

Father Gabriel Donato – report for De exorcismiset supplicationibus quibusdam, The Rite of Exorcism -subject, Sister Emeline of St Agnes's, Medcott.

On speaking with Sister Emeline of the Convent of St Agnes, in Medcott I have concluded with great attention and consideration, that she is not possessed by any demon that she speaks of. Initially her harrowing account left me in no doubt that the incubus she so confidently curses was the author of all this wretchedness that she has suffered. She clearly does speak in demonic tongues, that of which I have not heard in all my years of unholy possession.

Her future is uncertain, catholic doctrine permits me to disclose her story to you, Sister Magdalena, Abbess of St Agnes's, and, as such, make clear my finding before I submit my final report to his Holiness Pope Pius IX on my return to Rome. Please note the story you read is exactly as Sister Emeline relayed it to me. I have removed the profanities, something she seems unable or unwilling to control.

On the day Sister Emeline left the convent she explained to me of having feelings unfitting for a sister. These are of no concern to me, and do not put her faith into question, she simply wanted to pick sloe berries that she could see high up from the belfry and that were in abundance on Blackthorn Hill, behind the convent.

She explains, "I left the convent through the door in the walled garden. I had no intention of going far, but before I knew it, I was in amongst the large yew trees, surrounded by so many bountiful blackthorn bushes. I had picked many sloe berries, our crop of black berries at the convent had been dismal this year, and the sloe makes a very nice jam. As I walked back to the gate, something struck the back of my head. I fell into the undergrowth. I felt such weight pressing down on my back, my head held flat against the brambles, their thorns cut into my cheek. I was powerless. I could hear the tearing of my habit, and then the demon entered my body with such force. I tried to move Father. I used all the strength I had. I twisted my head to the side, the thorns cut deeper into my face. My vision was blurred from the blow, but I could see the jet black hair of this demon, his puffed bright red breast and the smell of his foul acidic breath. He finished his evilness and was gone. I was numb Father, and am now cursed. I have denounced this demon every day, but as you can see I carry its spawn, is this not possession of my body and soul Father?"

The father`s report continued.

After I finished my findings, all the facts did lead me to a conclusion, Sister Emeline had left the protection of the convent and in some way left her faith open to this depraved act. I would need more time to investigate before committing to any religious intervention. I had eaten quite late at the coach-house, and needed some hot water before retiring to bed.

I entered the bar and asked if the landlord could possibly heat some water, he was very obliging. The bar was packed with workmen, many covered in white chalk dust. My presence had gone unnoticed as when I travel or undertake an investigation outside of Rome, I am permitted to wear less formal clothing. The landlord gestured to me that the water was ready.

As I reached across the crowded bar, I caught the arm of a tall gentleman, he turned, his angry face squared up to me,

"Don't mind me friend, but watch my bloody ale!"

He started to laugh in my face, his breath pungent with the smell of ale, thick black greasy hair, he stepped back, and there under his coat a bright red waistcoat.

"Let me buy you another sir, by way of apology, I'm Father Donato."

"If you insist Father."

"And you are?"

"Willard, Willard Adams."

I was in no doubt that this foulest of men was Sister Emeline's incubus.

There is no comfort to be taken from my findings, the sister is a victim of earthly rape, neither can I condemn her belief that she is plagued and marked by the demon incubus. I also cannot report this Willard Adams without bringing the Basilian order into serious question. I leave with you the difficult arrangements that you must make regarding the unborn child. Please assure Sister Emeline her innocence, faith and devotion to God is not and will never be in question.

I was floored. The dirty bastard, Joel's womanizing father had raped a sister, my father's words rang true "Lock it up, or Willard will knock it up."

I continued to read the final pages of the journal, turning each page with trepidation.

"As Abbess it was my reluctant duty to God and to poor Sister Emeline that I should tell her of Father Donato's findings and that there was no demon or possession of which she speaks. She went silent, for the first time in months. She was once again the quiet gentle sister I knew before this tragic incident. She seemed to accept what the father had written, but late that night in her cell, she started whispering, whispering to someone invisible to all but herself, this continued right up to the birth on the fifteenth of September 1867.

The labour was very short, but painful, she whispered frantically, throughout, and in the early hours gave birth to a boy, quite small considering her size, and to our shock an hour later a second boy was delivered. Both were healthy, Sister Emeline was drained, but continued to whisper unfathomable words, she slept most of the next day.

We had already made arrangements for the babies to be adopted. This had been kept from Sister Emeline, along with our arrangements for her to be moved to a convent in Scotland, when she was fit enough to travel.

She eventually awoke very late, the night of the sixteenth. Sister Mary had received two mothers from the village in need of help with childbirth, a Mrs Chetwood and Mrs Kemp, the sisters had already delivered one baby, and they were in the final stages of the second delivery, within the hour both babies had been born. A few minutes had passed, when we heard screaming from Sister Emeline's cell, I unlocked the door and tried to comfort her, the echoing sound of crying babies could be heard throughout the convent, she screamed and screamed "Give me my babies."

I could not tell her that they would be leaving the convent in a few days for a new life. She had suffered so much, and was so weak and pale. I left to get some water, my thoughts were consumed with pity. On my return Sister Emeline had gone.

I could hear the faint sound of the sisters calling from the courtyard. I ran with great haste and as I arrived the sisters were pointing toward the belfry, some crying, others praying, and there she stood, Sister Emeline, high upon the tower teetering on the edge, clutching her tiny swaddled babies close to her chest. She kissed their heads and stepped off into the darkness. Sister Mary opened the gate from the walled garden, we ran through the unkempt grass and brambles to the base of the belfry, there lying in the undergrowth was Sister Emeline's lifeless body, still clutching her tiny babies, and there from the darkness just beyond poor Sister Emeline, crouched a solitary figure, its neck and arms twisted, bloodied, unnaturally reversed, it slowly rose snapping its contorted limbs back into place. Its face covered in the same pure white reversed wimple that Sister Emeline had worn to hide her shame. This wretched creature that stood over her, identical in every way, reached down and pulled the babies from Emeline's lifeless arms, held them close to its face for a few seconds, its shoulders dropped as if it pitied them, then with a frenzied rage threw them against the convent wall, picked up Sister Emeline and snapped her like a twig. It stood there, tilting its head side to side. Although faceless it sensed our holy presence, blindly observing us as if we were there for its amusement.

We knew then that Sister Emeline's accusation and condemnation of incubus had invoked this demon so foul to destroy that which he never created. The incubus's sole purpose to mock the Immaculate Conception, to miraculously impregnate then take back its evil spawn, but she had summoned an innocent demon, if there be such a thing.

Sister Emeline, a victim of human sin, Willard Adams' lustful depravity. Her empty possessed shell turned and walked into the darkness. We returned with haste to the safety of the convent, it would be difficult to explain to the sisters what we had seen, but we needed to make preparations for the body of Sister Emeline, and her dead babies.

As we entered our small chapter house one of the mothers from Medcott that had given birth earlier was frantically shouting "Where is my baby! Can I hold my baby?"

Sister Mary gestured to me, her face full of sorrow. She leaned over and whispered. "Sister Emeline took them."

In her anguish and sorrow she had taken the newborns delivered that evening, and unknowingly stepped into the darkness leaving her twins behind. It was my decision alone, and my weakness, that saw the women from the village return home embracing Sister Emeline's baby boys. Although twins, they were very different in appearance.

Every day I denounce the thing that left her broken, her body now buried high upon Blackthorn Hill. She lies in unhallowed ground beneath the blackthorn bushes and their sour sloe berry fruit that she so desired, cradled under each arm the innocent offspring of Mrs Chetwood and Mrs Kemp, no right can mend this wrong.

I hope our daily prayers can shield these two boys from what fate awaits. The demon within Emeline's tortured soul, and its deceitful whispers, the undeniable rage we witnessed that sorrowful night, unknowingly duped as it coerced Emeline to her nefarious leap of faith, her possessor unaware that the lives she clutched were not kindred.

I have lost hope as I write these final words. That creature, the fragments of poor Sister Emeline's soul, her anguish and devoted faith, trapped and controlled by an incubus of her unfortunate and unwitting making.

Father Donato had already returned to Rome; we had no choice but to furnish him with the events of that night and one month later we received our reply.

He writes...

"Of the entity you speak, if it truly is an incubus, it will follow her boys until the death prescribed is fulfilled. Its focus will be the first born and once he falls into the darkness from which he unknowingly escaped, it will continue its diabolical game, to finish that which it did not start. Sister Emeline a bride of Christ and unwilling mother will be the incubus's instrument of doom until that which she so openly but wrongly accused sees fit to end its game of vengeful retribution, my prayers and God's blessing go with you Sister Magdalena.

Father Gabriel Donato.

I placed the book back in the bag; the sun had dropped below the horizon, the evening light mixing with the moon's brilliant glow. I walked back to the inn, my mind overwhelmed with so many thoughts.

Willard Adams was my father, Abner was my brother and Joel, my half-brother. We all shared that man's vile blood and up there on Blackthorn Hill lay the bones of mine and Abner's unwitting mother, alongside Mrs

Kemp's and Mrs Chetwood's unnamed and unknown babies. Abner and I, separated by one hour, our death decided the day we were born.

I could now understand his fear of insanity, and Ellie, his poor stand-in mother, had her arguments with the unseen, actually been this spectre. This uncontrollable, unstoppable entity, which plagued him all his life, and my nightmares of being buried, now made sense, it was our intended end. I now felt widowed from the life I'd lived.

Nothing will change the memories of the only mother I knew, and then I suddenly remembered the story, as mother lay weak on the convent steps the night she gave birth. She saw the shape of a twisted figure standing in amongst the sharp blackthorn bushes, trapped by its barbarous thorns. It stared at the convent walls, waiting for something. Waiting for its accuser, Sister Emeline.

The inn was still empty, "Large brandy please landlord, the good stuff."

I sat near the open fire, and fed the meagre flames with Abner and Milly's letters. In the wrong hands these would serve no purpose to their memory. I kept the journal of Sister Magdalena, and Father Donato's report, I figured, as Abbess of St Agnes's, her story would need no validation in the right circles, and Father Donato's report was further proof that added credibility to an unimaginable story.

I finished my drink, packed up my gear and rode my motorcycle up to Valley Point. I left the bike near the road and walked along the ridge to the flat moss covered stone overlooking Medcott. The convent was way off in the distance, but resplendent on the horizon, as if the moon's sole purpose was to announce its hallowed structure, and the fortitude of its occupants, and rising up from the village, the darkness of Blackthorn Hill, the genesis of all this suffering.

Our first encounter at thirteen came flooding back to me. The nun we saw that afternoon, the remnants of my real mother, Sister Emeline, and her nonsensical message that mother was waiting.

I eased myself to the end of the large flat rock, and sat with my legs dangling over the edge, indifferent to the one-hundred-foot drop to the valley floor. I felt like a child once again, the light of the moon had never looked so serene, the air was still. I could sense that Sister Emeline, my unwilling mother, was near, no more than a broken marionette brought to life by her angry and malevolent ward, the incubus, its sole purpose, revenge.

I was tempting fate, sitting on the edge, but the night was so peaceful, and the only sound was that of a nightingale. This thing had spent a lifetime playing its games of torment with my brother Abner, finally convincing him to step out of that 4th floor window. Was it fear or destiny that occupied his final thoughts, I feel I would soon find out. His nightmare is over and I am to believe that mine begins. The entity would continue its game of fear and death, according to Father Donato, I have now become its prey.

I knew she would come this night, and as the hours passed, the night became silent, the darkness started closing in all around, and just before the sunrise, I could feel her sitting beside me. She gently held my hand, a warm and loving embrace took hold of my body, I did not resist. She was alone. I tried and tried to turn and face her, but something so powerful kept my eyes fixed toward Blackthorn Hill. I felt no evil presence, it was if she wanted to say goodbye, and as the sun appeared above the horizon she was gone, I know her next visit will be my last. Whenever or wherever, together we would fall into the abyss, along with her demon sentinel, no atonement would satisfy this creature, and so I close this story and hope my mother's waiting will soon be over.

Father Martin had a look on his face that I can't describe, so I won't, but he, like me, had a head full of questions.

"What happened to Mr Kemp Father?"

"A few days after I was supposed to meet Joseph Kemp in the Britannia Inn, the newspapers reported on a story of a well-respected London tailor, found naked and murdered at the front of the Gunthorpe Hotel in Whitechapel. It was later to be recorded as death by misadventure, so you see I failed him then, and now it's up to you to tell the world the real story."

Father Ambrose slowly looked across to the window, his eyes wet with tears, it was if he was saying you can take me now. He released the last few pages from between his fingers and they fell to the floor. The sun dipped below the horizon, and the room grew dark and cold. Father Ambrose closed his eyes and as the sunlight dimmed further the warmth and life from his presence soon left the room.

VIII
Willard. J. Adams

Joseph Kemp
Bespoke Tailor,
New Burlington Street,
London.

September 16, 1921.

*T*o *whom it may concern, this letter that you find upon*
my dead body, will without doubt identify the thing
that prescribed my end. It freely walks the streets of London,
frequenting drinking houses of the lowest kind, its influence
on those beneath its cunning intellect, of which there are
many, follow it with depraved devotion, a horde of shameless
parasites eager to please. It has no regard for anyone or
anything, other than its own self-preservation. It has escaped
from any kind of punishment for countless sinful, odious and

vicious acts against the innocent and naive, it was the catalyst for my beginning and the author of my death.

If not already in the hands of the police, I ask the reader of this letter to make haste and deliver it to the Whitechapel constabulary for scrutiny and I implore all detectives or any agent of the law to not be taken in by this thing. It will exhibit acute brilliance when cornered, its lies are its only truth. To go beyond its deception you must infiltrate its infected and corrupted world, show no weakness or vulnerability as this will feed its prowess. Think like the beast and you will triumph, a trait I did not possess. Tread lightly but tread confidently, you will find this foulest of creatures at 35 Hoxton Square, Shoreditch, its name... Mr Willard. J. Adams.

"Open up, open up now. One more minute constable then I'm taking this door apart."

"Hold on sir, I can hear something moving, there, did you hear it? Police, open up sir."

"I'm coming, I'm coming, you fucking idiots, you do know what time it is?"

The inspector growled back "We are well aware of the time."

He stopped short of returning the suspect's profanity.

I knew that this abrupt and early start would not bear well on the rest of the day to come.

The door slowly creaked open, standing in the hallway was a tall man of quite advanced years, his hair was long and the colour of slate, there was a strong smell of macassar oil, combined with stale tobacco, the edges of his once fancy but now well-worn cravat stained with the oily residue of the smelly coconut infused oil.

My father had used macassar oil all his life, he like his father, were both almost bald by thirty, but continued to use the hair preparation on the wisps that did remain, all strategically divided to cover his baldness. Macassar oil was the bane of my mother's life, whatever his head came into contact with, you would see the greasy marks and that smell of rancid coconut, so the odour was unmistakable.

The suspect was also wearing an old faded waistcoat, not unusual, but it appeared to be the kind a huntsman would wear. Buttoned high, remnants of its bright red hue could still be seen amidst the dirt and grime. An old healed scar ran from below his ear along his upper cheek and stopped just short of his left eye, its rough appearance indicated it was not stitched by the hand of any surgeon.

I couldn't help but follow its path to his dark lifeless eyes, his expression almost like that of a sightless person, disconnected, a slightly raised stare, as if he were looking over us. Across the bridge of his nose was a fresh cut, he'd made no attempt to clean the blood away, and the bruising around his cheek was an obvious sign that he'd been hit, and with some force.

"Are you Willard J Adams of 35 Hoxton Square?"

"Who wants to know?"

"I'm Detective Inspector Galbraith, and this is WPC Nichols, Leman Street police station."

"Well, well, London's finest, and a pretty little lady constable to boot, the streets of London will be safe now."

"If you could just answer the question sir, you're in enough trouble as it is."

"Is that so, well you just keep your drawers on, little bossy bitch tits and remember you're the ones disturbing me at this bastard hour."

"I would seriously advise you to watch your mouth sir."

It was clear he had not been to bed, fully dressed at six in the morning, and still wearing his coat and long boots, the inspector always encouraged the asking of the obvious, he believed it led the guilty into thinking you were clueless.

The inspector turned his back on the suspect, winked and with a dip of his head disappeared along the corridor making no effort to silence his studded boots on the uneven floorboards, the wink was my signal to ask the elemental questions. Galbraith had already sized up our suspect and saw no threat in his demeanour, just an old rude man.

"Do you have a habit of sleeping in your clothes sir?" I asked.

"Sir? You're so bloody polite, and posh, your eloquence missy just about hides the dregs of an East End girl."

He then took a deep breath, sniffed the air, directing his gaze at my legs, slowly lifting his head, his lecherous expression fixed, unchanging, as if his face were that of a waxwork cast.

"Very fragrant, on heat are we bitch tits?"

His foul intimidation was not going to deter me, but the inspector`s return would be more than welcome at this point.

"I'll ask you again, do you have a habit of sleeping in your clothes sir?"

"Depends missy, do you want to find out?"

It really wasn't my place to ask questions, Galbraith rightly or wrongly had this idea that if questioned by what he referred to as the calm squad, or women police constables, a more truthful answer would prevail. Our suspect was no different to the majority of corrupt men that I would encounter on a daily basis, be they young or more senior, the majority of them thought very highly of themselves, and especially those who had made a career of evading the hands of the law. The East End was full of individuals who seldom got their hands dirty, they would engage the services of desperate foolhardy down-and-outs, willing to make a few bob, the worst that could happen was a stay in Pentonville, or Belmarsh prison. They got a cell, a bed and food.

The real perpetrators had astute lawyers that knew every loophole, Galbraith despised them and their crooked legal representation, paid to fabricate alibis with ill gotten money, they were referred to as gentlemen criminals, but they were far from gentlemen. They merely saw us WPC`s as mothers, wives or whores in uniform, the latter, a reference to a failed clean-up operation, the idea was for female constables to impersonate prostitutes and then locate them across the East End`s most vice ridden areas, many arrests followed, a list was made to name and shame the men. One warning would be given and then their names would appear in print in local newspapers. They believed by targeting the clients and not the girls, they could rid the East End of just one of its immoral trades.

It was unsuccessful, no newspaper would print the name of any distinguished or respectable gentleman, which made up the majority of the arrests. These girls were driven by poverty, and not lustful urges, unlike most of the men, who treated them with violence and contempt, finish their deeds, toss the coins in the street, and then return home to their wives and families.

We did have the ability to calm a situation, hence Galbraith's nickname, but it was obvious to many that we posed no threat and their lewd responses a testament to their indifference to a uniform worn by a woman.

I had only been at Leman Street police station for a year. I was one of many female recruits who had finished their training in 1920 and was the only one from my class assigned to Leman Street in the summer of that same year.

Four long years of the Great War had taken the lives of an unprecedented number of men, depriving families of fathers, husbands, brothers and sons, and an incalculable deficit of manpower in all industries and occupations across the empire and this was the primary reason women had been given the opportunity to seek a career within the police. But I wasn't here out of need or necessity, my own guilt and despair had played a part in me pursuing this line of work, as well as a string of unrelated events.

It all started in July 1914, Austria declared war on Serbia and by early August the whole of Europe and Great Britain were at war. Within a few months I had enlisted and was serving in the Women's Army Auxiliary Corps. I was assigned to the War Office in Whitehall, my post began in late December 1914.

My role was as military driver, attached to the Directorate of Military Intelligence. I had a very good knowledge of London's streets, my father had spent most of his life as a coachman on horse-drawn growlers, and then from about 1903 driving the new motor car cabs. As a child I would spend all my free time with him, tending to the horses and then riding in the crawl space under the coachman's seat, I could see out but I couldn't be seen. At every stop he would call out to his fare paying passengers, 18 Langdale Street madam, or 2 Brick Lane sir. I memorised landmarks, famous buildings and monuments and then connected them in my head with the accompanying street or road. His passengers would usually be leaving the East End of London, heading to much nicer and more affluent parts of the city, so I would see London's beautiful architecture all illuminated by gas light, fog prevailing of course, and then get back home late, to the wrath of my mother, but father took most of the grief. She would wait up, but made a point of turning all the lights out, so it appeared she had gone to bed, as soon as father opened the door.

"So, you'll be getting Grace ready for school in the morning Arthur Stokes? No, I didn't think so, I can hardly wake that day-dreaming girl when she's had a good night's sleep."

Although they bickered at each other constantly, they were happy. Mother washed and ironed linen for well-to- do households, roping me in when it came to folding sheets and curtains and father would deliver them back to the big fancy houses, picking up a fare or two on the way back. My mother always wanted a girl, she would make pretty frocks and bows out of the fabric that some of her clients were throwing out, it was quite obvious sometimes that I was actually wearing a curtain, fashioned into a dress. Father wanted a boy, and to some degree they both got what they wanted. I hated dresses and bows but I would wear them, as if they were overalls, over the top of my britches.

Mother soon realised my passion was the day dreaming adventures with father and his two horses, Steed and Mabel. They were stabled within walking distance of our two up two down terraced house in Aldgate, which was actually Spelman Street, Whitechapel. If asked, father would always say we lived in Aldgate, even the working-class folk had delusions of grandeur, Chelsea or Kensington maybe, but he was convinced Aldgate was a league above the grimy streets of Whitechapel.

Every few days my chores would include cleaning and preparing the tack and tending to any injuries Steed or Mabel sustained on the unforgiving cobbles of the city's smaller streets. My pretty frocks would soon bear the scars and smells of stable life, and quickly found their way back into my mother's wardrobe and saved for Sunday best.

Father thought if I could master my way around London, I could be earning a wage as soon as I left school, but my passion for horses and my daydreaming days eventually waned. I was thirteen years old when father came home in a thing called a Prunel, a French made motor car. Steed and Mabel had served us well, so father kept them on for a few months and then sold them to a landowner in Surrey, they would end their days in front of a plough and harrow in the clean air of the countryside. He felt guilty for selling the horses, but I knew we couldn't feed and stable them and pay for fuel and repairs to the

Prunel. He taught me how to drive the motorcar in a matter of days, and how to recognise when things were not quite right. I soon understood the finer points of the combustion engine, the colour of its exhaust fumes and if maintenance was required.

He drove his Prunel motorcar cab for three years right up until his death in 1906, aged fifty-one. Over thirty years of sitting on his horse drawn carriage breathing in London's filthy smoke rich fog, had taken its toll and his lungs just gave out. Mother followed a year later and regardless of their bickering, she had lost the only man she had ever loved, her heart just stopped.

I was seventeen when she passed in 1907, homeless and without work. Unbeknownst to me my mother had spoken to the housekeeper, a Mrs Withers of Grave Dean House in Fulham, one of her biggest clients, and all a few weeks before her death, she had secured a live-in post in the employment of a Baroness Molston, without a word of it to me, it was as if she knew she had little time left. I'd never been the sentimental type and never had a boyfriend, so the only love I really knew was that of my mother and father. It's only the past few years that I can really say, I now know of my mother's pain and loss and I truly believe she died of a broken heart.

I took up my post at Grave Dean House, a most unusual and queer occupation. My role was to help the eighty-year-old baroness to wash, dress, and assist her at mealtimes, she had suffered a stroke and was unable to use her right hand and had limited function in her left, the rest of the time, I was to read, out loud, a selection of books, pamphlets and the evening gazette. The books would vary, from Jane Austin, Dostoevsky to Voltaire, mornings would be filled with poems from Wordsworth, Keats, and Robert Browning, who she constantly berated as I would read, his words could be quite risqué.

"Obscene frivolity has no place in poetry." She would say.

She would never stop me reading, her guilty pleasure I suppose.

The afternoons were devoted to the classics, and the evenings the London Gazette. Her tongue could be vicious at times and she was apt to falling asleep mid-sentence, her favourite game though, if you can call it such, was to allow me to read a full chapter, and then take great pleasure and amusement in my wrongful pronunciation of certain words. Her memory was sharp, and so it was that I would have to re-read the whole chapter.

"There is no such word as wor..ta, Miss Grace Stokes, it's water."

Seven years as Baroness Molston's helper, driver, reader and reciter of all things literary, had turned me from an East End girl to someone who not only sounded posh, but who could also hold a conversation with any of her ageing high society bridge playing companions.

Once a week on a Wednesday the baroness would forgo her breakfast allowing me to set out very early in the Rolls 40/50 or Silver Ghost as it was known, to an address in Belgravia, collect lady Soames and her party of bridge playing companions, and deliver them to Grave Dean House. They would cater for the baroness`s needs during Wednesdays and the rest of the day was mine, with a strict proviso that I was back before six o'clock to return the ladies back to Belgravia. Six o'clock was the end of my free day, and usually the end of their composure, and the sherry.

Her death at nearly ninety saw me become the household chauffeur to her only surviving and estranged daughter, Lavinia Molston. We had built a good friendship over the years, I was the only communication between Lavinia and her mother, and when war broke out Lady Lavinia saw fit to give me the freedom to follow my natural instinct to help and assist and do my bit for the war effort. And before I knew it my passion for motor vehicles saw me behind the wheel of a large military green Vauxhall D-type within the Women's Army Auxiliary Corps.

The army vehicle depot was located at the rear of the War Office in Whitehall. It was very similar to a taxi rank. We would wait until called and then be given a location by the adjutant, for either the collection of an officer, or to drive one to a specific location. One of my regular passengers was Lieutenant Henry Nichols, he was a military courier, a gentle soul, intelligent and very sociable, and although conversation was not permitted when carrying war office personnel, he couldn't help himself. We became friends very quickly, which led to our first dinner date, after that we met on many more occasions, afternoon tea, dances at the Savoy, and supper with his mother, Lady Nichols. A beautiful woman in mind, body and soul, who I am sure could see my lack of upper-class breeding.

Baroness Molston's uncompromising lingual transformation of me from an East End caterpillar to a society-sounding butterfly so to speak, positioned me well above my working-class status. I was neither posh nor poor, but in polite circles no one questioned my humble East End beginnings.

I was falling in love with Henry, barely did I think about the war that raged across the channel, and within six months we were married. Henry couldn't bear the thought of me driving all those rude stuck up war office types, so I gave up my early mornings, late nights, uncomfortable uniform and replaced them with delicate couture, society dances, soirées and all the trappings of an officer's wife. I had become a lady of leisure.

As the war progressed Henry's call to the front line was unavoidable. His role continued as courier to the War Office, but instead of London traffic holding him up, the obstacles were far more dangerous; bullets, bombs, mustard gas, and a bleak landscape littered with the dead.

Every day I would sit and wait for the post to be delivered, it had been weeks since I last heard from Henry, so when the War Office letter arrived, I opened it with great haste. To the floor fell a small amount of dried earth, followed by Henry's identification tag. I read that first line that so many had read before me.

"It is my painful duty to inform you that a report has been received from the War Office notifying the death of Lieutenant Henry Nichols."

Six weeks after Henry left for Europe, I was alone, living, no, existing, within a class structure that seemed for the best part oblivious to what was really happening across that small stretch of water and of the carnage in France and Belgium.

Henry's mother, Lady Nichols, a most agreeable woman and widower herself, insisted I move in with her. Even before we married, she was well aware of my working-class beginnings and made no issue of it.

Her journey from Miss Lucy Crabtree to Lady Nichols, although contrasting, was a comparable case of class-elevation. The late Lord Nichols, Duke of Wansborough, had fallen head over heels in love, after seeing her in Pirates of Penzance, she played the role of Mabel in an 1880 production at the Opera Comique in Westminster. He attended every night he could. It was noted in the London Gazette that the Duke of Wansborough had occupied his theatre box a number of occasions for the very same production, and with every performance his love grew stronger, convincing himself it was Miss Crabtree he had fallen for and not her character Mabel. He finally introduced himself backstage, and a romance ensued, the young duke's frequent attendance had earned him Miss Crabtree's affections.

The Nichols men must have a certain charm, as they were married that very year, three months after meeting and set up home in a large house in leafy Highgate. The house was adorned with photographs and paintings of Miss Lucy Crabtree's colourful career, and although Miss Pankhurst and her movement had done great things for women's suffrage and equality it would be a long time before the hypocritical upper classes would accept the wife of a duke treading the boards, or any occupation where they would excel in shadowing their husband and controlling their own destiny. I had only given up driving for the war office, Lady Nichols gave up a life in the arts, so I had nothing to complain about.

Not a day passed without a painful reminder that Henry was not going to return. I felt abandoned, I entered the world of high society on Henry's arm, our social divide never a point of topic, but now I felt an imposter. I may have been the widow of an officer and a gentleman, but I was bereft of his love and his noble ancestry, I was once again the daughter of a coachman from a grimy Whitechapel terrace.

Lady Nichols did not see class the way I did, maybe when you're at the top looking down you have a degree more empathy. I like to believe there was a small fragment of the much loved and adored performer Miss Lucy Crabtree still within, her deportment, her pronunciation was immaculate, maybe her greatest role to date. She was not a conventional dowager, in the privacy of her London home. She would address all staff by their first names, she had a heart that saw through elitist protocol, something her fellow peers brandished like a knife. She always introduced me as her companion and confidante, it was her strength that nursed my heartbreak.

One year to the day, after Henry's death at Passchendaele, November 6th, 1917, a name and date I could not forget, I decided to leave all my comfortable high society trappings and pursue a life that would bear no resemblance to my cosy and apathetic existence. Lady Nichols understood and helped me secure a mews property in Whitechapel, the area in which I spent my formative years up until leaving home for Grave Dean House in Fulham and three years later here I am, a constable at Leman Street police station, learning my craft from Detective Inspector Erskine Galbraith. I wasn't seeking atonement, but I was searching for a sense of responsibility.

My duties were limited, as a female constable, but Galbraith was an ageing dinosaur of a man, his judgement flawed by the bottle. I was sort of his eyes, ears and insurance, his retirement was looming and his pension at risk if he continued to miss vital evidence, as he had done on two previous but very prominent investigations, all before I had joined.

He had worked on some of London's most notorious crime cases, as far back as 1880. He never discussed his victories, he left that to everyone else, those who really knew him, of which there were few, believed his success was tainted by clandestine and illicit methods. Now I was privy to his vast knowledge of detection, not only did he think like a criminal, if his judgement was clouded by his addiction to Scotch, he also acted like one. I wouldn't say he took me under his wing, for at times I was his wing, and he knew, like many at Leman Street, that my diligence was all that stood between him and his full pension.

"What is this all about?" For the second time Galbraith raised his voice. "Are you Willard J Adams of 35 Hoxton Square?"

"This is 35 Hoxton Square and yes I am Willard Adams, so you can pat yourselves on the back, you've solved another case, now fuck off and let me get back to what I wasn't doing."

"I strongly suggest you restrain your miserable obnoxious mouth Mr Adams, does the name Joseph Kemp mean anything to you?"

"Well, that all depends on what he's claiming."

"Just answer the question Adams."

"I don't recall anyone with such a name, what's he look like?"

"He's a smart tailor from up west, and someone a judge would believe. Where were you last night between the hours of 9 pm and 3 am?"

"Let me see, the Britannia, on Dorset Street."

"Until 3 am? Spitalfields is a long way for a drink, especially at your age."

"I had other business to see to."

"Did anyone see you at the Britannia?"

"No, it was completely empty, like the Marie Celeste, I helped myself to the spirits and the contents of the till and then left without a trace."

I could see Galbraith's anger building; in the past year he had struck several suspects that showed little or no respect to his or my questioning. Willard Adams must have been in his eighties and a strike from Galbraith's club-like hands would not end well. He squared up to Adams, unfortunately he lacked the height of this ageing dandy, and Adams, very aware of his cocky attitude, dropped his shoulders, yielding to the inspector's inefficient encroachment, Galbraith aggressively whispered. "Don't fucking think about leaving London old man, we're not done with you."

Adams turned his head to look at me, he smiled and ran his tongue across his top lip, it was disturbing, as if he was unaware of the fifty or so years that separated us. This lewd gesture from any man would have been vile, he then spat at Galbraith's feet, turned and walked back into the lodging.

He left the door open, almost to say he had nothing to hide. I peered in and could just see the outline of a small dark figure, or what looked like a figure. The interior of the room was very dark. It moved quickly like the wind lifting a lace curtain, Adams peered round from the main room, he could see the inquisitive look on my face.

"You seen enough bitch tits? Now shut the fucking door."

Galbraith had already headed back to the street, he never took a shot of whisky in line of sight of anyone, but you could guarantee once provoked he would drink.

I didn't mention that there may have been someone else in Adam's lodgings, the deceased Mr Kemp had only cited Willard J Adams as the perpetrator of the murder, so at that stage we had no need to investigate further.

"Sir, you didn't mention the letter."

"Did he appear in anyway nervous to you Nichols?"

"No sir."

"Anyone can write a letter with accusatory content. I don't like that crude loathsome man, but we can't send him to the gallows on the words of a dead man. Remember the Musgrove case Nichols, the sweet little wet nurse above suspicion, with a string of baby deaths, all seemingly natural."

The Musgrove case was my first investigation with Galbraith. The rate of child death had increased in an area known as the Rookery, a city slum in the heart of the West End. It turned out that Mrs Musgrove, a popular wet nurse in the area and our very first suspect, was the only link to all the mothers of the deceased babies. She had been employed for a crown a child by these desperate mothers who could hardly feed themselves let alone their children, to taint the milk in such a way that the infants would slip away peacefully and without suspicion.

Mrs Musgrove was very nervous and jittery and almost confessed before we even questioned her, Galbraith had the ability to make even the innocent nervous, and although she was guilty as charged, his logic of first encounters wasn't always the most scientific.

"First rule of first contact, see what you're dealing with, now we know who he is and where he is, and to some degree what he is."

IX

"How far to the Britannia, Nichols? We need to see if this obnoxious man's alibi holds water."

"It's only a quarter past the hour sir, I doubt we'll get an answer."

"Let me worry about that."

If only that were the case, the inspector had an inventive way of making people take notice, and not always within the law.

We arrived at the Britannia public house, by foot it was a good twenty minute walk. Galbraith hammered on the door, using the bone handle of a knife he always carried concealed under a flap inside his coat. It was attached to a strong brass chain sewn into the lining, and although I had not witnessed it, the story back at the station was that Galbraith could flip the knife like a gunslinger, from handle to blade in the blink of an eye. He was always primed, ready to strike if a surprised suspect came at him armed with a weapon. It was not police-issue, hence the cloth flap that kept it concealed.

After about five minutes or so he grew impatient, this was usually the first sign of his unpredictability. We walked around to the back of the premises, Galbraith pushed his shoulder up against the large oak door and with a few grunts managed to lever it open. Along with his club-like hands he also had the shoulders of a rugby player and made light work of most locked doors. The entrance to the rear of the building was blocked by large empty ale casks. He rolled one precariously under a small window that was slightly ajar and untied a piece of oily rag that was tied to the handle of a sack trolley. He then climbed onto the ale cask, reached into his inside coat pocket, drew out an old half-smoked cigarette and a box of Bryant and May matches, placed the cigarette in the corner of his mouth, struck the match and lit the stub and without any hesitation proceeded to light the rag before the match went out. Once it had caught, he lowered the smouldering rag into the open window. It soon produced a great cloud of thick acrid smoke that filled the room, and then billowed out of the window into the yard.

Within a few minutes the sound of door bolts could be heard along with a muffled string of profanities, the door flew open and a half-dressed shoeless man tip-toed out onto the rough cobbles, followed by a plume of smoke.

"What in God's name are you doing?"

"Are you the landlord of this establishment?"

"I am, who the hell are you?"

"Inspector Galbraith, WPC Nichols, Leman Street Police Station."

"Are you not supposed to uphold the law? We do have a bloody front door."

The landlord looked quite shaken. Galbraith's methods didn't sit well with a lot of his colleagues, and it was frowned upon within much senior ranks, but Galbraith got results. Even with his fails, he still put more criminals behind bars than any other detective and was pivotal in London's most despicable ending their lives hanging from a rope at HMP Pentonville. He didn't have a boastful bone in his body but managed to make the Leman Street elite look incompetent, even with the simplest of cases.

I would never know when his improper use of police power would come into play, his face, his demeanour, gave no clues to what he was thinking or what he was about to do. Complaints were commonplace when it came to the inspector, and we would both face the same cautioning from superintendent Meadows for his capricious techniques. After our ticking off he would explain how Meadows had got to be superintendent, it was safe to say that they were not friends or colleagues. Superintendent Meadows was desk bound and strictly by the book, Galbraith's desk was as messy as his principles, he thought like a criminal, and that is how he prepared me for London's under-belly.

"If they know you're the police, you will get no respect."

They usually did know, as I was always in uniform.

"But if they see you breaking the rules it confuses them, if they think the truncheon up every copper's arse isn't being manipulated by the chief inspector then maybe this copper is alright."

I had experienced his ability to put the guilty and the innocent on the back foot, it was not my place to say if his rationale or philosophy was flawed, but Galbraith's presence was intimidating enough without any of his erroneous antics.

The inspector was of medium height with broad shoulders, slightly stooped over, until something caught his attention, prompting him to unfurl his casual but bear-like stance. His stature reminded me of an old framed woodblock print of a bare-knuckle fighter my father had hanging in the hallway. He'd taken it from an London Illustrated News that someone had left in the back of his carriage. It caused many an argument, as my mother hated it. She would have to pass it every time she went out and on her return. The caption read "James Mace, World Heavyweight Champion 1863", my father would just call him The Gypsy, that's how he was best known to his audience. He had become quite a celebrity before the Marquess of Queensberry introduced gloves and a set of rules to what many had considered a brutal venture of the lower classes.

"What's the point of fighting if they have to wear big stuffed mittens," my father would say.

My mother's hatred was directed more at my father than that of the almost naked James Mace holding a defensive fighter's pose. He had carefully cut the page from the London Illustrated News and inserted the woodblock print of The Gypsy over the top of a rather draconian and austere looking photograph of his mother-in-law. She had died long before I was born and by all accounts, according to my father, the unforgiving and miserable photograph exhibited all of her best points.

Galbraith, like Mace, also sported a large handlebar moustache, and on the right side of his face was a deep port-coloured birthmark, it was the first thing you saw and from a distance looked like blood on his face. It disappeared under his moustache and continued down to his chin. His face was unmistakable and unforgettable.

His father, a well-respected watchmaker from Glasgow, moved the family to London when he was only eight years old. His Scottish accent had all but disappeared and the only real connection with his homeland was the whisky that coursed through his veins. He wore a long black faded coat, matching waistcoat, and high lace-up boots. His look was comparable to that of a working class man's Sunday best, the cut and style of his jacket was of Victorian appearance.

His face was expressionless, and few situations would change that, but when angered he was like a lion. His movement was slow and calculated, mainly due to a gunshot wound he sustained years earlier, then he'd pounce with no warning and before you knew it, his large hands would be clamped around a suspect's neck, suspended, their feet barely touching the floor, and as they slowly turned blue, gasping for air. It was obvious that his methods, his drinking, his hidden madness and everything he stood for was inherited from an era long since passed, his irregular practice was as outdated as his Victorian attire.

The potential to learn from inspector Galbraith was as dangerous as it was vast, and the reason the faceless hierarchy that had placed me under his mentorship was twofold; his retirement would see a rise in unsolved crime in the East End, and no other constable had lasted more than a month within his company. So, as it stood, my almost full year had seen a significant drop in complaints against the inspector and the station.

Although physically uncouth in his handling of what he called miscreants, he was very polite around me. He was no angel, he would only swear if he thought I couldn't hear him, but I still had no idea what had led him to this prominent and at times destructive career at the Leman Street station in Whitechapel.

"Do you know a Mr Willard. J. Adams?"

"Everyone knows that snake."

"Was he here last night?"

"He and his cronies are always here, at the beginning of the week and at the end of the week."

"So, who are these cronies?"

"The East End's worst blaggers and chancers, Willard is like a modern-day bloody Fagin to them."

"What time did he leave?"

"I don't know."

"Try and remember sir, was it busy last night?"

"Not particularly."

"Was there anyone with him you didn't recognise?"

"Let's be quite clear inspector, I know Willard like I know my own shit, and I have no desire to take any interest in his dealings. He's a punter, I serve the ale, the punters pay me and as for his so-called disciples."

"Disciples?"

"That's what they call themselves, his clan or den of thieves, he's well known to all the scumbags as the jack of all trades, not one of them legal, but your lot have never managed to send him down. I've been landlord here for over thirty years, he and his verminous rag-tag disciples have been around for as long as I can remember, all smelling worse than my slop trays. They've never done an honest day's work in their lives."

The landlord's defamatory comments made it obvious that we had not been mistaken regarding Willard Adams` character. Galbraith glanced at his pocket watch, I could see he was losing interest, so at this point I had to intervene.

"So nothing out of the ordinary happened last night sir?"

"Few fights, broken glasses, spilt ale, the usual, constable."

"Any of those fights involve Willard Adams sir?"

"Well, there was one incident, a very well-dressed gent came in late."

"Around what time sir?"

"I really don't take any notice of the time, I opened up on the dot and I closed on the dot."

"What did this gentleman look like sir?"

"Fancy tweed jacket and waistcoat, pocket watch, gold mind you, not the usual gun metal. He asked for two glasses and a bottle of malt whiskey and sat in the corner."

"Two glasses? Did someone join him?"

"No, but he kept looking over at Willard's table, which in itself is an invitation for trouble. The next thing I knew the gent is up, standing in front of Willard and his clan, he said a few words, and then threw a book right at Willard, caught him on the bridge of his snout, he must have hit a vein, as the blood gushed everywhere."

"Did you hear what the gentleman said to Mr Adams?"

"No, but I think they knew each other."

"How so?"

"Well, Willard stood up and said, 'Go on, keep on following me son, and I'll slit you open, gut you like a rabbit and drop your remains out of the window.'"

"How is it you can't recall the time, but you can remember what Adams said?"

"I'll slit you open, gut you like a rabbit and drop your remains out of the window, it's his favourite threat, heard it more times than I care to remember."

Galbraith looked across at me, as if to say, see the calm squad theory works, we would have reached this point eventually, even without me doing the questioning.

The landlord had nothing to hide, but at least the inspector`s face was doing that rare thing of re-engaging.

"I need a time."

"Like I said inspector, I don't watch the clocks."

"Guess man! Beginning, middle, end of the night, was it dark out, were the streets lights on, you know when to open and you know when to close, so which end of the night was it?"

"It was dark out, so if I had to guess, maybe ten o'clock."

"Did the gentleman leave straight after the incident?"

"I wasn't really interested in the gent, Willard's cronies looked set to take the place apart, so I had to calm them down and kick them out."

"So, you didn't see the gentleman leave or Mr Adams?"

"No."

"And this book the gentleman threw at Mr Adams?"

"I picked it up and put it behind the bar."

"Can we see it?"

"You could if I still had it."

"What happened to the book sir?"

"Another chap came in, asked if I had seen his friend. He said he was running late and that they were meeting here. I assumed that Willard's spat was with his friend, so I explained the situation. He then asked if the gent had left something for him. I said yes, two glasses of malt, unpaid for, and an old book, so he coughed up, and I gave him the book."

"Can you describe this second gentleman sir?"

"Well dressed, well spoken, but he wasn't quite right, well not for this pub."

"How so?"

"The dog collar was a bit of a give-away, he wasn't trying to hide it, but his scarf and coat collar was covering most of it, he seemed quite at ease amongst the scum and ex-cons that drink in here, but he did have a familiar look about him. He actually reminded me of someone, can't put me finger on it though."

"Did you get a name sir?"

"No, I got my two-bob bit for the whisky, he got his old book, and left. He could be Jack the Ripper for all I cared, so if you're quite done with me officers I'd like to get some kip before opening up."

"If Adams is in tonight, not a word sir."

"What's the degenerate done anyway?"

"That, we don't know yet?"

X

We returned to Leman Street, it was still very early, Galbraith put a fresh pot of coffee on to boil. He made it to a standard that was undrinkable by most, but it was the perfect camouflage to the cheap whisky it would be laced with, no smell of alcohol escaped his old tin mug.

"Nichols, get Manston to drive you to Joseph Kemp's premises, there may be some clues there, New Burlington Street, wasn't it?"

"Yes sir, what about Adams?"

"I'll deal with him later, after I speak to the Gunthorpe Hotel, someone must have noticed something odd, although I wouldn't put it past Adams to push a man out of a fourth-floor window, not even a totally naked man, but I doubt he'd have the strength, and he didn't strike me as dimwit."

"Do you think he had help sir?"

"Maybe, and leaving the victim clutching a letter that would see him hang, also seems foolish."

"He may not have seen the letter in his hand sir."

"If you throw someone out of a window, someone naked Nichols, I'm sure you`re going to notice something other than the obvious. Go and see Manston now, tell him it's urgent and I sent you, he can wait in the car, you know what he gets like when he leaves the station."

Albert Manston was a retired detective, Galbraith's partner for many years. He'd been shot during an active break in, which later turned out to be a staged robbery. It was common knowledge that Galbraith always took the lead on everything, on that ill-fated day Manston took the lead. He didn't require Galbraith's battering ram shoulder, the door was unlocked, and as Manston entered first, the gunman just opened fire, the first bullet passed through his cheek shattering his jawbone, just missing his brain as it exited the left side of his face. Manston would tell the story as soon as he saw someone looking at his irregular shaped jawbone and large butterfly scar.

"If I hadn't turned my head at that split second, Galbraith would have been wearing the contents of my head."

Although he joked and liked to brag, his facial disfigurement was indisputable evidence of an unembellished story. The second bullet hit Galbraith in the hip, and still resides there now, both bullets were intended for Galbraith. The gunman fled and was later caught and gave the names of everyone involved. The inspector had made enemies of a lot of people from the criminal fraternity to corrupt civil servants, that was the first and last attempt, and one of the reasons Galbraith always carried his concealed knife.

Manston didn't come off so well, his ability to detect after that was all but gone, he couldn't even open a cupboard door without flinching. Galbraith used his influence to keep Manston on as a driver and administrator of police records, he had saved his life by catching the first bullet, and Galbraith repaid that act. He knew headquarters would force Manston out of the police, along with a paltry half pension. Manston was officially retired now, but Galbraith kept him on, his presence and duties in crime records was a procedure no one wanted to do. He and the inspector were the last of the nineteenth century breed that bent the rules to fit, so he was retained with no questions asked.

"Take the next left sir."

"How do you know these streets so well Grace? And I wish you would just call me Albert."

"My father was a coachman sir, if I wasn't with the horses, I would be under his growler seat memorizing streets and landmarks, and the inspector doesn't advocate first names during working hours sir."

"That's what you think. He's not the same ogre when you're not in the line-of-sight Grace."

"There on the left sir."

"Where?"

"Just below Brooks, the milliners."

Manston stayed in the car, he was no longer in possession of a valid police warrant card, this prevented his involvement with suspects or witnesses, to add to that, the shooting had left him mentally scarred. He would joke about his facial injury, but he had an absolute fear of any new buildings, doors and alleyways that were unfamiliar to him, so his driving duties suited him down to the ground.

The shop was situated down fifteen or so noisy cast-iron steps below street level. Although it was a basement shop the front window was large and quite impressive, rolls of brightly coloured fabric were laid out in a plait in the front of the shop window. Standing on a shelf to the right was the top half of a mannequin wearing a bright red officer's dress jacket, above the window was a delicately hand painted sign, 'Joseph Kemp Bespoke Tailoring' this could be seen from the street, slightly obscured by the ornate black spiked railings.

The shop door was slightly ajar, a small card plaque hung on a chain visible through the single pane window, "CLOSED". I pushed on the door, it was quite stiff and as I forced it the door made contact with a high pitched entry bell, the ringing soon faded away to the sound of a whirring, which I guessed was a sewing machine.

The inside of the shop was actually very small, divided by a heavy looking green velvet curtain, two more full length mannequins stood at the far wall, both dressed in fine tweed suits. The large bay window to the front of the shop had a thin layer of dusty grime covering the upper panes diffusing the mid-morning sunlight.

I approached the green velvet curtains, the whirring sound stopped, I called out "Police, is there anyone in?"

A few seconds passed, then two small pale hands appeared through a gap in the curtains, grasping them and pulling them back. There in front of me, a small lady wearing a brown pinafore dress, adorned with pins and needles of all sizes, pieces of ribbon and braiding clipped to her sleeves. I said good morning and introduced myself, she glanced at me and gestured to come in, turned and walked back to her sewing machine.

Some of the light from the shop filtered through, but only enough to see this was an even smaller room, the lady sat back down and turned up the wick on a large oil lamp on the work-bench.

"It's Joseph? You're here about my Joseph?"

"Yes Madam, it is about Mr Kemp."

"Tell me, is he hurt?"

A dreadful and dizzying feeling of nausea filled my body, I could see and hear myself reading those raw and numbing words again "It is my painful duty to inform you that a report has been received from the War Office notifying the death of Lieutenant Henry Nichols."

That impersonal War Office letter, written with stoic sorrow, but lacking any regard, comfort or empathy for the recipient, and now I was faced with delivering this terrible news and worse still I could give her no specific details of Mr Kemp`s broken naked body, lying there on the street, his cold hand unwilling to relinquish the letter identifying our only suspect.

"Can you tell me your relationship to Mr Kemp?"

"I am Mrs Kemp, his wife."

"I am sorry to inform you that Mr Kemp was found seriously injured in the early hours of this morning on Gunthorpe Street, outside the Gunthorpe Hotel, his injuries sustained from what we believe to be a fall. The night watchman found him during his rounds, a doctor from the Royal Hospital who had lodgings at the Gunthorpe was awoken and attended to Mr Kemp, but his injuries were beyond the doctor's expertise and Mr Kemp died before the ambulance arrived."

Mrs Kemp`s hands began to shake, her head wavered as if she were to faint. She grabbed my arm to steady herself, her small gentle face holding back a mournful tear and then with a hesitant cry she clasped her head into her hands and sobbed.

I felt her pain, her world would suddenly become a smaller place, every memory would now be like the pages from a book, a never changing story that would fade with every passing year. I tried to comfort her, but grief such as ours, or hers, is isolating. Your mind becomes absent and conversations are fragmented, no words can comfort. My heart was filled with empathy but my head knew Galbraith would want a full report, and her pain could get no worse, and though she shook her head with defiant disbelief, she knew her husband would not be coming back.

"The night watchman reports Mr Kemp managed to say one word, Emeline, would that be you Mrs Kemp?"

"Sister Emeline, that was his mother. Poor Abner and now my dear Joseph, they both perished the same way, the same place, he knew it was coming."

"Sorry Mrs Kemp, what did he know?"

"His death, he was convinced it would be this day or that day, two years he waited."

"Waited? Was he unwell Mrs Kemp?"

"Only with a sickness he couldn't see or fight."

"We are following a lead, and we do have some evidence of foul play."

"So, you have the journal then?"

"No, but we are aware of its existence, but not to its whereabouts or its contents."

"It's ungodly and unthinkable I know, but I'm glad, I'm glad his suffering is over, that evil pig Willard Adams is to blame for all this misery, my poor, poor Joseph."

" You know Mr Adams?"

"We have never met, but I know the pain and anguish he caused Joseph, his lies, his deceit. I lived every moment these past few months trying to share Joseph's burden. At first he couldn't find him, and when he did, Willard just laughed in his face."

"What business did your husband have with Mr Adams?"

"He is Joseph's father."

Mrs Kemp continued to tell me the most extraordinary story, not only of her husband, but that of his brother Abner and of a great darkness that followed them both, there was also a third brother, Joel, all three were brothers, but totally unaware of their kinship and the blood that connected them. I listened intently and noted down as much as I could. She explained the authenticity and truthfulness of the journal and that it would not be questioned, as it was written by the hand of Sister Magdalena, Abbess of St Agnes's. This vital piece of evidence would be imperative to making Willard Adams answerable to its despicable content.

"Mrs Kemp, do you think Mr Adams would harm your husband?"

"He was not his executioner of that I'm sure, but Joseph's blood stains his hands and his cold heart and blackened cursed soul."

"When did you last see or speak to your husband?"

"Yesterday evening, around six o'clock, he took the journal, he knew Willard's address and where he usually drank. Joseph was in such a melancholic frame of mind, I tried to persuade him to confront Willard in the morning but he insisted this was the last time and that the journal would put an end to his father's lies."

"Did Mr Adams acknowledge that he was the father?"

"He denied everything, the existence and the contents of the journal. Joseph had me write the relevant parts in a long letter and we posted it to Willard Adams. Joseph was so fearful that Willard would just burn the journal and all the evidence would be lost."

"Do you know if he read the letter?"

"Oh, he read it, they met a few weeks back. Adams made it clear the only bastard he had sired was his feral son Joel, who he had not seen for forty years and last night Joseph was to confront him with the indisputable evidence, that of the actual journal."

"Was your husband planning to meet anyone else last night, Mrs Kemp? The last place he was seen was at the Britannia public house, the landlord mentioned your husband asking for two glasses."

"Once a year he would get word to Joel and Abner so that they could try and meet on their birthdays, you see they were all born the same night, Abner's sad death was two years ago to the day. When Joseph returned from

Abner's funeral he too became infected by the darkness that plagued Abner's mind. He only had Joel left now to turn to but he was usually absent from their reunions due to his foolhardy ventures that saw him in and out of prison. I am of the opinion that both Joseph and Abner were tormented by something unnatural. Yesterday was the 16th of September and although you cannot tell me constable I will speculate that my poor poor Joseph lay naked on that dimly lit shadowy street and not far from where his brother Abner lay dying, two years earlier."

My mind began to race down conflicting avenues, the dilemma was how much of the supernatural did I include in my report and had I just misinterpreted the words of a woman whose heartache had only just begun, a feeling that I knew all too well.

Before leaving I asked Mrs Kemp if she had someone she could stay with. Having experienced the sorrow and pain on reading that my Henry was not coming home, I knew the feeling of her irreversible loss. She had a sister in Camden Town, I took the address and left her there in that dark empty workshop. I could hear her sob as I pulled the door shut, a lament that was all too familiar.

On my return to the car, Manston was fast asleep, his addiction to alcohol was far more severe than that of Galbraith's, and unlike Galbraith, Manston couldn't conceal his alcoholic dependence, he either slept or slurred, he seldom embarked on any work without the engagement of some sort of intoxicant. The records department was located in the basement of Leman Street, he pushed pieces of paper around all day, unless he was required to drive myself or Galbraith somewhere. The inspector could no longer drive due to the bullet lodged in his hip from the gunshot wound ten years earlier. It would have been safer all round for me to drive, but Manston needed to appear useful, filing records was just a masquerade, and required only a few hours a day and no real intelligence, certainly not that of a detective sergeant. Albert Manston was known as the sleeping dog, and the best place for him was below ground and out of sight.

XI

We arrived back at the station late morning, detectives and constables acting on case inquiries had the privilege of entering the station through the back entrance, avoiding the steady flow of crooks, drunks and loose lipped wretches either on their way in or out of the station. It was a five-storey building and could hold a considerable number of suspects for questioning and those that had been charged awaiting their appearance in front of a magistrate. Another of Galbraith's drinking associates was duty sergeant Banks, his was the first face you would see entering the rear of Leman Street.

"Good morning constable Nichols."

"Morning sergeant."

"Your bull is in the china shop Nichols, you might want to try and work your magic."

There was no magic, I had no control or influence over Galbraith's moods, he despised uncouth and ungracious behaviour around women. If he saw any detectives or constables acting in a boorish manner, he would single them out, then make sure everyone was listening.

"Every copper needs a Dr Jekyll and a Mr Hyde, you won't catch a cold, let alone a miscreant without both, but in this division and in this building Mr Hyde does exactly as his name suggests."

There was an unmeasurable contrast between Galbraith and Detectives Simmonds, Renton, Staves and Howard, all of whom occupied the top floor along with Galbraith. The four were known as the Leman Street elite, a title given to them by the London Newspapers, not related in any way to their conviction rate, but a reference to their Eton and Oxbridge education, Galbraith called them dicktectives. So I had no desire to break the illusion that they thought I had control of his inner beast, the gentle man within his hardened frame was always present when I was around.

After typing up the morning's report I was eager to get Galbraith to take a look, the Imperial typewriters issued to the station were not without their faults and reports would be slow to transfer from the scribbles in our small notebooks. I finished late that afternoon and placed the four pages in front of the inspector.

"Anything out of the ordinary Nichols?"

"You better have a read sir."

He would normally read a few lines, glance up at me and say. "This is very descriptive, Nichols, but just give me the essentials."

Not today, he continued to read all four pages, running his finger along as a guide and mouthing each word silently as he read.

"So, let's just get this straight, Nichols, our man Mr Kemp, returns home to his childhood village two years back, buries his good friend a........ Mr Abner Chetwood, who he later finds out is his brother and at the same time discovers his real father is the obnoxious Willard J Adams, and his real mother being that of a catholic sister, where is it, oh yes, Sister Emeline, who was raped by Adams. She gave birth to twins and in her grief threw herself off the convent belfry along with the two babies who she believed to be hers, but were actually born earlier that evening in the convent to Mrs Kemp, and Mrs Chetwood, women from the village of Medcott. The sister's tragic mistake left her and two unrelated babies dead at the foot of the convent, whilst her actual babies lay in the cloister awaiting adoption. The abbess hatches a plan to cover up the dead sister's distressing blunder, and with, I'm guessing divine intervention and wisdom, gives the two women from the village Sister Emeline's babies, fathered by none other than Willard J Adams. To that the newly widowed Mrs Kemp believes that Mr Chetwood and her husband Mr Kemp were tormented by an unknown but inhuman presence that only they could see."

"Yes sir."

"I'm not finished yet, constable. Then Mr Kemp is found naked and left for dead on Gunthorpe Street, having fallen from the fourth-floor window, the very same window that his newly found brother, Abner Chetwood, fell from only two years earlier.

"It reads like something Mr Poe would write."

"Poe?"

"You know, Edgar Allan Poe."

I was well aware of Mr Edgar Allan Poe, and of his writing, Baroness Malston would not allow his words to adorn her extensive library shelves, she would express great distaste if such a book were critiqued by her bridge group.

"His words are too fantastical, and his horror all too theatrical."

I didn't see Galbraith as a reader of any kind of publication, the Gazette maybe, and the way he mouthed every word silently, eyes guided by his finger along every line, must have been tiring. Although Galbraith would seldom be impolite around me, whenever he did read a full report, he was accustomed to reading it as if it were Sherlock Holmes taunting the guileless Dr Watson, and who could blame him. As I typed it that afternoon I felt as if it was a far-fetched story straight out of a Penny Dreadful publication.

"Strange as it may seem Nichols, Adams has just disclosed the same story to me, different wording, different context, he's conveniently removed himself as the aggressor, but his fanciful story points the finger at Mr Kemp."

"And the rape of Sister Emeline?"

"He was quite adamant that he had no need to force his, let's call it manhood, as his words were too vile, on any woman. If they were in his company, they were asking for it. He went on to say that Mr Kemp was threatening to take proof to the police and after last night's spat at the Britannia he did follow Mr Kemp out into the street, to tell him to cease with the harassment, in so many words."

"Did he acknowledge any of Mr Kemp`s story?"

"Yes, he said it was utter lunacy."

"Do you believe him sir?"

"Tell me, what do you think, Nichols?"

My unqualified and inexperienced position led me to believe Adams was the murderer, but I knew that Galbraith always expressed doubt if all clues pointed in one direction.

"Everything points to Adams sir, motive, opportunity."

Even as I said the words I could feel the blood rising to my face. I had provoked a smile out of the inspector, which was not easy, the kind of smile a grandparent gives a mischievous child.

"Nichols, that's what I would expect from the detective elite."

I continued to add to my embarrassment, and so wished I had presented my report without the questionable and ambiguous dark entity.

"It does all look quite conclusive sir."

"Yes, it does Nichols, if not for one thing."

"What would that be sir?"

"Mr Kemp`s letter appears to be genuine but also very misleading, but a very clever way to condemn a slippery serpent like Willard Adams, and what better way to send an enemy to the gallows. But it won't hold water Nichols, it's dated the 16th of September, which either means Kemp killed himself, or he knew the day he would die, we both saw his injuries this morning, and those hands were not going to be writing anything, so that rules out dating the letter after he had fallen."

"So you don't believe Adams could have done it sir?"

"It grieves me to say it Nichols, but no."

"Not even with the total disrespect and the atrocious attitude that Adams exhibits."

"Unfortunately, he has no conviction record anywhere, I checked every file, although there is a Joel Willard Adams, and believe it or not Willard owned up to fathering this lad Joel back in the 1860's, although he relinquished any fatherly responsibility thereafter. His wife, yes, he had a wife Nichols, who he discarded, his very words, discarded. He went on to say, 'She loved that little shit, more than me, her own husband, by the time Joel had reached ten my wife's engaging body had gone the same way as her fishwife mouth. I left him in that shitty little village of Medcott in the welfare of his unappealing but devoted mother. So, you say my boy`s doing a stretch in Pentonville?' I responded, 'He's no boy, he's in his fifties now.' To which Adams replied. 'Fucking retard.'

"This is what we are dealing with Nichols, no record, no respect and no empathy, and we'll get nothing from Joel Adams. He has served 30 years on and off in Newgate before they raised it to the ground, and was last serving a ten-year stretch in Pentonville for aggravated robbery, but with parole he could have been out for quite a few years now, so it appears the same poison runs in the Adam's veins. So this second man, the recipient of the journal, may well have been the son, Joel Adams?"

"You`re forgetting the dog collar sir, our mystery man is a vicar or a priest, if the landlord can be believed."

"Maybe, but I don't trust the landlord one bit, his eyes or his mouth. And apart from all that Nichols, Adams has no idea that Mr Kemp is lying naked in the morgue. He believes Kemp has made an allegation of the rape of Sister Emeline, and that's it. Not once during my questioning did he mention anything that implied he knew of his death, or that he had any intention of harming Kemp, or to kill him for that matter, regardless of his very public threat at the Britannia.

"Manston, I need a file from the archives."

"What case inspector?"

I could see Galbraith was onto something and more importantly he didn't want me to know. It was something he and Manston would only be privy to, it was a simple deduction. Everyone knew if you required a file Manston was not the person you asked. His lethargic approach to the archiving of closed cases was at best slow and noticeably so. It was quicker to look yourself amongst the rows and rows of filing chests and archive boxes.

"Can I help sir?"

"No Nichols, I need Manston to dig out an old file, check it and then return it before anyone sees it's out."

"Something to do with the previous death at the Gunthorpe Hotel sir?"

"Much further back. Adams said something odd whilst I was questioning him, something only the police knew about from a very old case. I find it very surprising that Mr Willard J Adams has not crossed my path in all my years here, he's not someone you forget."

"Maybe that's not his real name sir."

"I did consider that Nichols, but then there's the story of his son Joel, I'm guessing the same name in a different order. I did query the J in his name, and got the answer I expected, 'Jack be nimble, Jack be quick, the girls all love Jack's candlestick."

"That doesn't surprise me sir, what did he say that was so odd sir?"

"If I'm right you'll find out soon enough, Nichols. As soon as Manston finds that file we'll pay Mr Adams a second visit and end this today."

XII

As we arrived Galbraith barked at Manston, "Stay awake Albert, we might need to bring Adams in, and I don't want to be beating you around the head to sober you up.

"Nichols I'm going up first, I'll need five minutes."

Galbraith knew I couldn't turn a blind eye, and my reports were an accurate record of events, so his five minutes were an out- of- sight deception, never seen, then it never happened. But the bruises, blood and, God forbid, broken bones, were undeniable proof, a reminder that he believed his unlawful means justified the end, and if he were right, it would mitigate any suffering that he caused. I waited by the car for a few minutes.

"Remember sir, Albert, remember what the inspector said, keep alert."

"Yes Grace, a hasty retreat suits me, I have a date with a bottle of Glenfiddich tonight, I don't think that bandy old twig Adams is going to cause Galbraith any trouble."

"Let's hope so for Adams` sake."

Willard Adams` lodgings occupied the roof space of the building`s top floor, two large dormer windows looked directly out onto Hoxton Square, one window was wide open. As I walked across the road I could distinctly hear Galbraith's raised voice, then the sound of glass breaking. I entered the building and ran up to the room, the door was open. I shouted through to the inspector, there was no reply. I edged my way along the wall of the short hallway, to the left was a small room, no window, a dirty toilet, and some old stained under garments hanging from a chord. A washstand stood up against the wall, sitting on top was a Gladstone bag, the type a doctor would use and a quantity of surgical implements were strewn all over the floor.

I shouted again, "Inspector!"

Still no answer. As I leaned forward I could see the lower half of Galbraith's legs, as if he were sitting on the floor, the door frame obscured my full view. I entered the room slowly, and was immediately overwhelmed with the smell of paraffin, the vapour was far worse than the pungent oily odour, and my eyes started to water.

The well-worn uneven parquet flooring glistened with pools of the liquid paraffin, a broken lamp lay in the middle of the sparsely furnished room. There was far more paraffin than that of a single broken lamp and there sat

Galbraith, leaning up against the wall beside the closed window, facing me, his chin resting on his chest. I could see he was still breathing, blood was running down his face from a wound above his eye.

The room appeared empty and then it hit me, a single ice cold whack across the back of my ankles. I could feel the warm blood oozing into my shoes, but no real pain. My legs collapsed and just before my knees hit the floor a hand grabbed my collar. I turned and looked up, it was Willard Adams. He held me there, suspended off the floor, my feet just hung loosely like that of a lifeless puppet. He lifted me up to his eye-line, his strength incomparable to any eighty-five-year-old man or any kind of man, he ran his tongue across his lip once again.

"We could have danced a merry dance, you and I missy."

He then released his grip, I fell to the floor, my shoes full of blood. I could see he had cut through both my Achilles tendons, a long bladed surgical knife lay in front of me. I reached for its handle, but there in the cold bloody steel I could see the reflection of a small dark figure on its mirror-like surface. I turned quickly, but nothing was there, the paraffin fumes and throbbing lacerations were playing tricks with my mind.

I dragged myself up against the door frame, my feet and legs were useless, I realised I was powerless to help the inspector.

"It's going to get a little warm in here missy, you might want me to relieve you of that drab uniform."

"Just you try it Adams."

"That sounds like an invitation missy, but don't flatter yourself. I like my girls to have a bit of get up and go, and you're going nowhere."

Adams walked over to the open window, took a deep breath, then struck a match and flicked it into the middle of the room, the paraffin ignited with an immense flash, most of it had now pooled into the centre of the room.

Galbraith was still slumped in the corner, Adams knelt down in front of him. He slapped him with such force his head recoiled against the wall, Galbraith's eyes opened.

"You filthy bastard Adams."

I knew the inspector's strength and tenacity was our only chance, but he never moved. I could see no reason why his past aggression would fail him now. He looked across at me, his face now full of regret, he then glanced down at his hands. Both palms were facing up and there, protruding from the centre of each hand, the heads of two large thick iron nails, Adams had nailed his hands to the floor. His legs were bent in a sitting position and through each boot was a single nail of similar size. Within the few minutes I had waited with Manston Adams had somehow overpowered the inspector, and managed to drive four nails into his hands and feet.

He was trying to talk, but I couldn't make out what he was saying, my vision, now impaired by the smoke, and the flames were distorting the sound. Adams then placed two fingers over the inspector's mouth and began talking to him. I could hear a few words, but nothing was clear.

"Calm down inspector, it's been a long time Erskine, you don't mind me calling you Erskine?"

"Who the hell are you Adams?"

"We don't have much time, well you don't. Cast your inept mind back, thirty odd years, dates, places, names, all memorised in my magnificent head. You were the young constable, strawberry jam scar all down your sorry sad fucking face, you looked like something from a sideshow act, sporting your cape and piss pot helmet, remember Buck's Row? Early hours of the morning, no? There was an old lamplighter, a drunk and his whore and me, we were all standing over the body and then you came running up blowing your whistle ready for action, a real bona fide copper. I stood right next to you, as you puked up all over your shiny new boots. It was the first time anyone had seen my handy work, and it was my birthday, August 31st 1888, not my best work admittedly, but I had to start somewhere and who better than little Mary Ann, and then you made your first of many mistakes. I remember your weak whiny voice."

"Did anyone see anything? someone must have seen something."

"Well, the drunk and his whore saw nothing, they both had had a skinful, and the lamplighter was blind and as mad as bat shit. My waistcoat was soaked in her blood, there's a reason why I wear red Erskine. As the crowd grew bigger, your snivelling asinine attempt at being a copper saw me casually walk away. I could smell your fear then as I do now, and so did Annie, Elizabeth, Catherine, Mary, so on and so on. So, you wanted to know what the J stood for in my name. Before I left shitty old Medcott, I was jack of all trades, then I parted company with that diseased place for this stinking city, the girls all knew me as Jack, Jack the lad. You see I had many fingers in many sweet pies, you know what I mean Galbraith? Then all the nice girls left, and the East End was left teeming with filthy whores. I know what you're thinking Erskine, they were nice girls once and maybe they were, more reason to set them free, you had your chance to stop me all those years ago, but you and the like were all incompetent oafs, and now look at you, an old relic, fucking your hand because no woman would have you. I doubt even your little miss tight cunt over there would touch you and to add to your inadequacies I sent your police commissioner a letter, just to help you out, then I grew tired, bored you could say. London's finest jumped into bed with the guttersnipe press and I became a sensation.

"Listen carefully Galbraith, here's your very last statement, so pay attention, the J is for Jack, the Gazette added Ripper and then every bastard fruitcake from Limehouse to Soho thought they were Jack the bloody Ripper. Oh, you sold newspapers, Erskine, I read the stories with great interest, but they missed one vital piece of evidence, the letter I sent your commissioner, never published that, did they? Oh, you could have had me in the very first instance at the very first scene. I explained in great detail what I had done on five occasions, and that I, Jack the killer, had stood right next to a copper with a strawberry jam birthmark all down his face, yes Erskine, it was you, but you're the great Galbraith now. I do hope in some small way I slowed the course of your career. Ripper, fucking Ripper, I bet you came up with that moniker, Jack the fucking Ripper, it has no finesse."

"You filthy savage bastard Adams."

"Now now, Erskine, it's a little late for name calling, well, for you anyway."

"So you did murder your two boys Joseph and Abner."

"My God Galbraith, here before you kneels the legend that is Jack the Ripper, the one that got away, the one you could have stopped. My deeds will see me live forever in the minds of those who crave terror and conspiracy and yet you concern yourself with the trivial deaths of my bastard offspring. You don't deserve the title of inspector, but if you wish to go to hell along with Abner and Joseph as your final case, and seek no interest in me, the greatest killer this city has ever, or will ever see, then so be it. Their deaths were not by my hand, the killer stands over there in the shadows, see her? There, in the corner, you probably can't, the torn habit, face always covered, it hangs around like a bad smell, I always got the feeling it's waiting for something, an apology maybe? The innocent little sister picking berries, innocent my cock, she gave herself freely up there on Blackthorn Hill, no struggle, no complaint, just blissful silence and to be frank my virility far outweighs her indignity. She's the only bitch I can't get rid of. All these years, she, it, call it what you will, has been somewhere in the darkness.

"At first it was quite off putting, and then I realised it had no business with me. It all fell into place when that idiot Joseph showed up with his journal. Fifty- odd years its followed me in the hope I would lead it to those two bastards I sired, and now its job is done. Fear not inspector, if you can't see it now, you will soon enough, especially where you're going, so when you arrive on the other side of life, say hello to all that scum I skilfully dispatched. And with that I'll bid you farewell Inspector Erskine Galbraith."

Adams stopped talking and opened his hand wide, fanning out his long bony fingers, he placed his thumb on Galbraith's chin, then proceeded to move his hands down the inspectors chest, as if he were using the old method of measuring the height of a horse. Adams then stopped around mid-chest and spat on Galbraith's waistcoat to mark the spot, reached into the inspector's coat and pulled out Galbraith's concealed tethered knife, carefully placed it on the spit and slowly pushed it through his waistcoat, inserting it right up to the handle. The inspector was motionless. Adams then punched the handle with great force, within a short time the blood was flowing from his heart with no resistance. His face turning paler as the life left his body, his head slumped over to the side, and he was gone, his eyes wide open, staring at me through the flames.

Adams rose up, put his back to the wall to avoid the flames then edged his way around to where I was sitting by the door. He looked down and stared at me, as if he was about to end my life.

"You can see her missy; tell me you can see her."

I could, behind him, a small dark figure. Adams turned, stepped over my bloody severed ankles, and exited through the door. The thing mimicked his every move, as if they were one, the door slammed shut behind them.

I twisted round to reach the handle, to no avail, Adams had removed it, he had left me and the lifeless inspector to the mercy of the flames. I knew if I could just get over to the window I could shout down to Manston in the street below. The fire was now travelling along the ceiling and down the walls towards Galbraith's body. I grabbed the corner of the rug and pulled myself along. I could feel the warm blood trickling from my shoes leaving a trail as I dragged myself along the uneven floor.

I managed to reach the bed, I rolled onto my back and pulled myself under by using the metal bars of the bed frame. The floor was littered with rust-stained surgical implements, small apothecary bottles, labelled chloroform, lined the skirting board under the bed. Interspersed were larger specimen jars containing perfect but terrifying dismemberment of female genitalia, trapped, preserved like trophies in a display case. I reached for the edge of the bed-frame and dragged myself through to the other side.

I finally reached the window, it was impossible to get any leverage in a sitting position. I reached across the floor and grabbed a small brass pot and hit the window several times, eventually the glass broke.

The heat had reached such a level that the bedding was smouldering, giving off a pungent and acrid vapour, burning my eyes and throat. My thoughts were with my Henry, his fear, his death, he must have suffered as I do now, as the mustard gas entered his lungs. There was little time left. I pulled myself up to the broken pane ready to scream down to Manston in the street below and as I did, a leather gloved hand grabbed my arm.

"We'll have you out in no time madam."

My saving grace, Whitechapel's fire brigade. I was carried down to the street below, Galbraith's body was also recovered, but by the time they reached him, the heat had fused the fabric of his clothes to his body, and for all their efforts they could not lay him flat, so they propped the inspector up against the railings, as if he would spring back into life, his face and hands cinder black, the iron nails still embedded in his boots. The remains of his old heavy coat were glowing like a well-lit cigarette, and there, across the street, sleeping in the car was Manston, oblivious to the carnage that had transpired during his scotch-induced slumber.

Adams and his creature were long gone. What I saw that evening was undeniable and incomprehensible and whatever he and the inspector discussed died within that blackened room. Joseph Kemp`s letter, and the only proof we had, now just embers in Galbraith's charred coat pocket.

I spent two months in the Royal London Hospital, the burns healed quite fast but my tendons are still a cause for concern. Later that year I was awarded the King's police medal, Galbraith was awarded a posthumous medal. The coroner`s verdict was less fitting for a detective of Galbraith's vast years of service and distinction, it was recorded as misadventure. The official report that replaced mine, read...

Inspector Galbraith and WPC Nichols entered 35 Hoxton Square, a fire broke out, started by an unknown assailant. Due to poor visibility the inspector lost his footing, fell and was impaled through the heart by his own knife that was concealed within his coat, the assailant then savagely attacked WPC Nichols before making his escape, no clear description of the suspect has been ascertained because of the poor visibility.

My full report, on Willard J Adams, Joseph Kemp and Abner Chetwood, was read by the commissioner and subsequently misplaced to avoid a newspaper scandal that the great inspector Galbraith had been murdered and myself maimed and left for dead by an eighty-five-year-old man and his demon accomplice. Manston was made a scapegoat and was officially retired in 1923. His role within records had been given to me until my injuries could see me return to active duty, but this time it would be alongside the detective elite.

Their textbook policing would see me duty bound to forget all that Galbraith had shown and taught me. They were the progeny of a cautious and new era of policing, it was the abhorrent ugliness of the Great War and the waste of life, my Henry's life, that propelled me from my elegant and lavish lifestyle to this desk in Whitechapel. I can now see the ugliness we all possess. Adams wore his like a cape, Galbraith's was within, only to surface when challenged by an adversary.

Adams, had challenged and conquered in a most horrific way, his freedom protected by fear of scandal. I sometimes wonder what other evils lie within that vile man's past and if only we had read Joseph Kemp's words in good faith.

"I implore all detectives or any agent of the law to not be taken in by this thing, it will exhibit acute brilliance when cornered. Its lies are its only truth, to go beyond its deception

you must infiltrate its infected and corrupted world. Show no weakness or vulnerability as this will feed its prowess, think like the beast and you will triumph."

FATHER AMBROSE
XIII

September 11th 1967

Dear Father Ambrose

I hope my words see you in good health in your one hundredth year of life. Some would think it hopeful folly to wish you many more returns, so I will just congratulate you and say enjoy your cake, you have earned a slice or two.

I shall take up my new post as parish priest in the small town of Cotting in less than a week, Father Fellows has now vacated the rather worn-down rectory house. His housekeeper Mrs Cooper passed away some years back and as of late he has been missing morning Mass, and at ninety years of age it's a rather unforgiving walk into Cotting. He has reluctantly moved into the comfort of Saint Christopher's house to see out his days, along with some of our other clerical colleagues.

Our Lord is most definitely in your favour Father Ambrose, as you have managed to elude the ardent care of those at Saint Christopher's and as you also have more than five years seniority on their eldest resident Father Daniels at age ninety-five, I would say without doubt you are blessed.

Once again, I wish you all the very best, I trust Mrs Hawkins will furnish you with one of her legendary bakes. I will endeavour to drop in on the sixteenth and drive you down to the village for a celebratory sherry before heading on to my new post, it's only a small diversion by car and will be a welcome one at that.

Your dear friend
Father Martin

"Happy birthday Father Ambrose, happy birthday to you!"

"Thank you Mrs Hawkins, a beautiful reminder that I have been stuck in this confounded wheelchair for another whole year."

"Can I see the telegram Father?"

"No, no Mrs Hawkins it's a letter from Father Martin, wishing me a happy birthday, he's dropping by later with the intention of buying me a sherry at the village pub."

"Does he know we have a cupboard full of the stuff here?"

"No Mrs Hawkins."

"You really do need to let the parishioners know you detest the stuff Father."

"It may be a little late in the day to start returning years of goodwill gifts."

"There must be twenty bottles of sweet sherry in that cupboard."

"Fear not, I have left instruction with the bishop, it will all be yours one day very soon and as I've seen you make very light work of that cooking rum that seldom makes its way into your excuse for a rum cake, you'll be more than set for at least a hundred trifles."

"Moan all you like Father, but I've never seen a crumb left on your plate."

"You very seldom get a crumb when it's that stodgy Mrs Hawkins."

"Very droll Father."

"I doubt he will stay for very long, but I need to speak to him on a very pressing matter, this may be my last opportunity before he's consumed with his new calling at old Father Fellows` parish. Fellows has been sent forth to that place that shall not be named."

"You mean Saint Christopher's House?"

"Bless you my child, once again you remind me of my trite destiny."

"You've never been there Father, you're afraid you might actually like the company of other priests."

"Yes, you're right Mrs Hawkins, I am afraid, afraid of spending my precious last moments discussing ecumenical issues with museum pieces, at the home for decrepit clergymen."

"Cheer up Father, one hundred years, that's an incredible milestone."

"My hearing`s not so good today, was that millstone?"

"You heard me well enough Father, and as for being stuck in that wheelchair, I see you sneaking out for a cigarette of an evening on the terrace after dark."

"I'll try and be a little more covert next time."

"If it keeps your filthy habit out of the house Father, struggle all you like to the terrace, but remember if you take a fall, it's Saint Christopher's for you!"

Mrs Hawkins was a wry sort, thick skinned and to some degree a bit batty in her thinking, she had tried for more than five years to get me into Saint Christopher's, knowing full well it would see her without an income. Or maybe my unfounded but unfavourable comments about the place meant she knew her destiny was to discover me dead one morning in my chair and in the house that she had managed remarkably well during our thirty years together.

Mrs Hawkins, like myself, grew up in the village, I returned nearly forty years ago to take up my last post, after spending ten years in London parishes. Mrs Hawkins had never left the village though, she was thirty odd years my junior, and not quite in her seventies, she could read my mood, most of the time. She was sharp and up to date on worldly affairs, our light hearted joshing was a double act that gave way to some quite serious conversation, and that in turn has kept my century old brain from hibernation, my body may have dozed off, but the marbles are intact.

"Do you have the telegram Father?"

"No, just some other cards from the parishioners, I'm sure her Majesty has better things to be going on with, and not to sound ungrateful, but I'm feeling a little exhausted with the whole one-hundred-year event, can you wheel me into the study?"

"Yes Father, will you be taking breakfast there? Or on the terrace?"

"Well, it's nearly eleven, I'll take some of that yellow stodge you're passing off as madeira cake and a pot of tea."

"It's lucky I know you so well Father, anyone else would have taken offence."

"It's a pity you don't take offence Mrs Hawkins, your hefty bakes may improve, I have actually read somewhere that they publish books on how to make the perfect cake."

"Cheeky beggar, you have a sharp tongue Father for a man of the cloth, I've said it before, and I'm sure I'm not alone in wondering how a man with your cutting but harmless wit managed to become a priest."

She wasn't mistaken in her thinking. Many had questioned my ordination nearly fifty years ago, and however strange it may sound, I am here because of three things; my mentor Father Fabian, an unholy ghost and a violent foul-mouthed man.

"Have I not told you of my odyssey to the priesthood Mrs Hawkins?"

"Indeed you have Father, and many a tale besides."

I had not always been a priest, my calling came in my fifties and many an eyebrow has been raised, of that I am certain. My passage at times was fraught with pious arrogance. I found that God does not judge us on earth, that is the role of the pontiff's lap dogs, those who take up office of the highest importance, their influence is beyond the counsel of the meek and poor, and they serve only those above them.

My ordination was a new start, to help, and to guide, I had no intention of rocking a boat that had long since taken on water. The Catholic church has changed little since my formation as a priest all those years ago. I have out-seen five popes and outlived countless priests and bishops, all many years my junior, and now I sit here in my one hundredth year, all because of a gentle priest who killed a violent man, then calmed a vengeful ghost.

"You are welcome to join us for a drink in the pub later Mrs Hawkins."

"I fear not Father, to be seen in the village public house drinking sherry with two priests, whatever next."

"Oh yes, your reputation Mrs Hawkins."

"Get on with you. How's this Father?"

"A little closer to the window, when Father Martin arrives just point him in the right direction, we have plenty to discuss before the day is out."

"Lucky Father Martin, but remember it is your birthday, so do take it easy."

"Very amusing Mrs Hawkins."

I had to stop giving Mass six or seven years back, the walk into the village became too much and Mrs Hawkins` driving was as close to purgatory on four wheels as I would want to experience. The rectory was quite a large house, and occupancy was guaranteed as long as my service was required, so although I could no longer take Mass, I could receive my flock for confession or religious guidance at the rectory. The take up was small, but it kept me from the clutches of St Christopher's House for cantankerous old priests, which I fear I was becoming.

The wheelchair was Mrs Hawkins` idea, and at first I despised the thing, but then I realised I could move two or three times the speed my legs could carry me, so I kept it. My legs work perfectly fine, just very slow and with the aid of my stick I can navigate the whole house and garden and more importantly, the terrace, for a cigarette.

"Good afternoon Father Martin, Father Ambrose is expecting you."

"Good afternoon, Mrs Hawkins, you're looking very well, it must be what, ten years?"

"I fear a little more Father, we seemed to have missed each other your last four or five visits."

"Life treating you well?"

"I cannot complain."

"I'm sure the good Father Ambrose does plenty of that for you?"

"That he does and with such dedication too."

Mrs Hawkins had a habit of conducting conversations in the porch. She did like to talk and knew as soon as a parishioner from the village entered my study for guidance or other church matters, the who's doing what in the village would be cut short.

"Mrs Hawkins, Mrs Hawkins, I'm sure Father Martin would like to sit down and have a nice cup of tea."

"Like I said, such dedication, down to the end of the hall, door on your right Father, I will make a fresh pot of tea, some cake, or a sandwich?"

"A small piece of cake would be lovely."

"Happy birthday Father Ambrose, you're looking incredibly well for a one-hundred-year-old priest."

"Yes, yes Father Martin and thank you, it's been too long, but I am very glad you came. I have some things for you and a confession I need you to hear, I fear this will be my last birthday at the rectory."

"Are you planning on your next to be at St Christopher's House?"

"God no Father Martin, but we need to make time, I need you to receive my final confession."

"I know your ways are a little unorthodox Father Ambrose, but I doubt the confession of a priest from a sleepy parish will take very long."

"It's a fifty-year-old confession Father, almost from the beginning of my journey from rags to these robes."

"It is well documented, the pauper that became a street urchin, from urchin to workhouse, workhouse to prison, and prison to priesthood, it's a story well told. You were the modern-day traveller, left out in the cold, stripped of clothing, a sinner, beaten, and left to rot so to speak, it's the story of the Good Samaritan, and the church was that Samaritan."

"I fear you have been reading too much Dickens."

"I will gladly take your confession Father Ambrose."

Father Martin was correct, my story was like no other. I was coming to the end of a prison sentence, I had been a thief of some description most of my life, right up to the age of forty or so; pick-pocket, house breaks, market stalls for food, I never laid a finger on anyone in anger, only self-defence. My final three years saw me share a cell with a defrocked priest, a Father Fabian, his crime, stealing from the church. Over the course of five years, he had managed to sell hundreds if not thousands of pounds worth of silver cups, plates and religious trinkets, all so his poorest parishioners could eat and clothe their children. Even today the Catholic church is blind to those disgraceful few that wear their vestment to disguise their shameful acts upon innocent children. But to steal from the church, was as if you stole from the pope himself and you would be left at the mercy of British law.

My crimes were selfish, I cared not for the victims, just my own pithy avarice. Father Fabian taught me a great many things, how to express myself without cussing, to articulate and be well spoken, inject elegance where there was none, to see people's pain, even if it was not obvious, have empathy for those who did not deserve it, and most of all, how to make my life count so I could help others.

My first encounter with Father Fabian was late summer 1917. I had to vacate my cell due to damp and was moved into Father Fabian's cell, on account that no one else wanted to share with a priest. His tiny west-facing cell window just caught the last remnants of the late summer sun and the first words he spoke to me were. "The beauty of a setting sun is hope enough that a new and better day will follow."

From there on he gave me guidance, and I gave him a degree of protection from those who had no respect for a priest, regardless of his crime. Although Father Fabian was defrocked, he had a good many friends who had seen his harsh treatment as unjust. He wrote a long letter of recommendation for me, and a list of priests I could turn to for help and guidance on my release in 1918.

I was presented as a would-be candidate at the Corpus Christi Catholic Church Maiden Lane in Covent Garden. I had to convince the parish priest that I had the making of a priest, then pass the scrutiny of the Director of the Ordinands. Of course, my character was deemed unsuitable, but my maturity at fifty distinguished me from all other candidates.

I somehow passed the scrutiny of the Ordinands Committee. I was told to spend six months working in the parish before I could be recommended for training, this I did with great enthusiasm, and in 1921 after three years studying Theology, I was ordained aged fifty-four as Father Ambrose.

XIV

"Tea Fathers, and a small slice of cake, I've made you a sandwich Father Ambrose, as you've already picked at my madeira cake."

"There is good reason for that Mrs Hawkins, it's madeira in appearance alone, as the good Father will soon discover."

"Thank you Mrs Hawkins, I'm sure it will be lovely."

"We will be heading down to the village at around five-thirty, if you would like a lift Mrs Hawkins. I need to pay a visit to the churchyard, should auld acquaintance be forgot and all that, and Father Martin has generously offered to buy me a celebratory drink at the pub."

"I do need to check a few things for the wedding next Saturday with the verger, so I will take you up on your offer."

"Where would you like to start Father? With your confession that is."

"Well, my rebirth or evolutionary development like you say is a story to tell, but there is an incident that taints, no taunts me. I seek disclosure, so when you tell my story again, you can just say I was a hopeless discontented man who found salvation and became a priest, who saved himself and a few others along the way, but not the world entire."

"You wish me to make your story a modest tale for misguided folk Father?"

Father Martin was an elementary kind of man, if there was good, it's opposite was bad, and if he saw evil, then it made sense to him that it's reverse was divine and holy.

We first met in 1930, when he took over the Parish of Islington as a fresh-faced priest in his late twenties. London's population had grown so much and it was close to fifty years since my first encounter with the city`s wretched underbelly, and its influence that kept me trapped in a loop of theft, prison, liberty, theft, prison, liberty. I knew that for my new vocation to make a difference at age sixty I would need a community that would seek the help I could give.

London needed more than religion, the church could not provide for those most in need, and the word of God could not fill an empty stomach or shelter the woeful homeless in London's most deprived boroughs and city parks, that was the failing of Ramsay MacDonald's national government in the grip of the Great Depression.

And so, I eased the young Father Martin into his post in the Parish of Islington, and after a year my application was approved to return to the area I grew up and to take up my second, but final post.

"No Father Martin, I would like people to see us priests as men, no more powerful or enlightened than any good soul that walks this earth. Too long has the pious, celestial hierarchy created this divine right of self-importance, a most disagreeable distinction of position versus belief, fuelled I might add by the bishops, cardinals and the pope himself."

"Careful Father Ambrose, there's a touch if not a pulpit full of heresy there."

"Sorry Father Martin, but as you well know my three years of training came hard, guided by Bishop Michaels, the only bishop who would recognise my dedication, but once ordained I was eventually accepted by all. As you know Father, I had been appointed to the parish of Islington, and my confession starts there. The church was granted access for a weekly visit to HMP Pentonville. I was a bit naive back then, but now it's obvious that Islington was an appointment no one would choose to take, poverty was rife and the prison engagement was thankless.

"You can imagine the immense feeling of pride I had on my return as a priest and not a criminal, no more could the guards treat me with hostility. The dumbfounded look upon their faces and the elated look of Father Fabian, my cellmate. Not only did he put me on the right path, but used what influence he had left within the church to see me start and finish my training, he had only a short time left before his release to a world that would offer him nothing but humiliation and stigma. I find it peculiar that you can start life as an undesirable sort and then make good, but in reverse and in the eyes of the church, you are forever untouchable.

"I was given access to the prison chapel, mainly to talk to vulnerable inmates, the elderly and those who feared their release after many, many years of incarceration. The prison governor would not allow services, words of hope could be bestowed upon those who awaited the rope, but not forgiveness. Confession was forbidden, even for those that were most repentant, I was not going to refuse these sorry individuals the right to confess and seek forgiveness because they were to hang and deemed beyond redemption. God alone has the last word on forgiveness, not the British penal system."

"That seems very fair Father, so you broke a few rules, we all have at some point."

"Confessions, forgiveness, blessings, that's not my confession Father."

"Sorry, please continue."

"A few weeks before Father Fabian's release, he was moved into a cell with an old man, he must have been in his nineties, charged with lewd propositioning of young ladies and of exposing himself many times in Hyde Park, and if his final victim had not been the daughter of a very influential KC, he would have continued, by all accounts, a rather distasteful character.

"I continued with my weekly visits, and group consultations, many just wanted to know what would greet them in the outside world. The first time I met Father Fabian's cell mate, was unnerving, he never uttered a word, but I knew that face, scarred and creased, eyes that burrow into a man's soul, calculating where their weakness lies. I'd seen it a hundred times before, every thief, swindler and killer possessed this look of treachery, a look I thought I had long since lost, but he could see it. My corrupted past neatly concealed within my priestly gown, my faith unquestioned to all but him. I know from my own experience that after a few weeks in prison, if you possess certain repugnant traits that your fellow convicts relate to, you soon find yourself admitted to the den of thieves. Your crime becomes your badge of honour and a nickname is soon to follow, they called him Jack the lad, make no mistake he was ninety if not a day, but he was strong. His real name, Willard Jack Adams."

"You remembered his name Father."

"His name, his face, his infidelity, is etched into my very soul. He would sit at the back of the prison chapel, repeating what I said, like a mocking-bird. Father Fabian had tried to reach him, as he did for me years earlier, but he was convinced that the man was driven by such evil as if guided by Satan himself, he would not dare undertake a rescue of this man's soul. At night he would stand naked over the father's bed urinating on him, laughing and talking to an invisible entity as he carried out his foul act."

"He truly sounds as if he is beyond help, surely he would have been better in one of the mental institutions."

"Please Father let me finish before I lose my train of thought."

"Sorry."

"His appalling deeds went unpunished and unseen. When confronted by the guards he would lie and just say Father Fabian has soiled himself again. He took the father's food and what he didn't steal he would defecate in. Father Fabian was convinced he was bedevilled, possessed. One night after lights out, Father Fabian could hear voices, that of Adams and one other.

"This became a nightly occurrence along with the urination and other degrading behaviour. Father Fabian couldn't make out what they were saying, they mumbled most of the time. It would go on for hours until the early morning light penetrated the cell, and then Adams would sleep in late, blaming, no accusing, Father Fabian of crying like a baby all night keeping him awake."

"The man sounds insane."

"During his final week Father Fabian requested a private consultation with me, this was a few days before his release. I must be clear now, Father Fabian was not a man to overreact, he had served as an army chaplain during the great war in the Balkans, he was witness to death and carnage, but when we spoke that morning, he was a frightened man, he had seen something, an entity or presence dancing in the shadows whilst Adams slept, he could not explain it. It sang the words, Ut animam suam, ut animam suam over and over again, he sat close to me and whispered the story as if the devil himself was listening. He believed his cell-mate Adams was in league with something depraved that hid within the shadows. He was not only convinced that he had to kill Adams but that he had to do it before his release."

"Ut animam suam? My Latin is not so good these days Father Ambrose."

"Ut animam suam, Take his soul."

"What did you do Father?"

"I managed to speak with the officer in charge, and to see if I could get him moved. I was told it was a very long process, and he only had days until his release. The officer was under the impression that Adams was a feeble old man. Adams had successfully made Father Fabian appear as the protagonist and the author of all his own suffering.

"I gave Father Fabian a book, its words written by a devout hand, words that were pivotal during times of doubt after my training as a priest. Father Fabian had showed me the way out of my miserable life, and all I had to do was to persuade him to make the right decision, he only had a few days left inside those walls.

"We spoke many times during those last few days and I had hoped my guidance would give him the strength to overcome this presence that mocked him from the dark and take control of his emotions.

"I arrived at the prison early on the day of Father Fabian's release and was ushered into the Governor's office. Mr Botting, he knew me well, first as a prisoner and now as a priest. He was softly spoken, but with a strong Yorkshire accent and an intermittent stammer.

"He was a very fair and just man, who seemed a bit out of place as the head of HMP Pentonville and although he had no religion to speak of, he did see some benefit in my work, if not only for the generous donations from the diocese. He had an astonishing ability to switch between my real name and my ordained name. Of all my brief meetings with him I spent most of the time correcting him, his stammer would allow me a few seconds to fill the silence with my name chosen by Bishop Michaels."

"It's Father Ambrose now sir."

"Of course, of course it is Father."

Bishop Michaels had chosen the saintly name at my ordination. Saint Ambrose spent his life in service to the unfortunate and although I wished to keep my birth name, as it was the name of a prophet, the bishop convinced me to go forth with my new calling and a new name. But on that morning Mr Botting was faultless, every word precisely spoken, no awkward silence, meaning I had no need to correct him.

I took a seat, and waited for him to finish his conversation with Dr Guthrie, head of the prison's infirmary. Mr Botting then explained how Father Fabian had managed to sharpen the end of his small wooden cross, a luxury he was allowed to keep, and whilst Adams slept, he had plunged it into the old man's neck, puncturing his jugular. The blood pooled under the cell door and was spotted by a guard before lights up. Father Fabian was found sitting at the foot of Adams' bed, crying, repeating over and over, forgive me Sister, forgive me Sister.

"You were not to know Father Ambrose."

"Father Fabian was convicted of first-degree murder and sentenced to death by hanging. Three months later they hung him."

Mrs Hawkins appeared from nowhere, an ardent eavesdropper, another skill she hadn't mastered along with her cake baking.

"I'm ready for my jaunt into the village Fathers."

She could see the atmosphere was charged, and God only knows how long she had been listening, but some fresh air and a change of scenery was most welcome and I think Father Martin was struggling to make sense of the last few minutes of our conversation.

The village was a little under two miles by car, we arrived around six, and at a pace more conducive to a man of my ripened years.

"Can you drop me at the church Father Martin?"

"My pleasure Mrs Hawkins."

"That will suit me as well Father, I need to pay my respects to a few below ground."

"Will you be alright to walk Father Ambrose?"

"Oh yes, he has a good two hundred or so yards in him each day, they're slow ones mind you, but he'll be fine with his cane."

"Yes, thank you for that Mrs Hawkins, always nice to know if my speech should ever fail me, I'll have you for back-up."

"Perhaps birthday boy needs his sherry first?"

"Father Martin you go on to the pub. We passed it as we entered the village on the right, and I'll meet you there when I'm done, it falls within my two-hundred-yard allowance, aye Mrs Hawkins."

I paid my respects to those I had outlived, at the age of 100 there were many, I then made my way slowly to the pub. The village was very quiet for a Saturday, some clouds in the sky, but a lovely warm September sun.

I eventually reached the pub. Father Martin was outside looking out for me, we went in and sat at a table near the window.

"I took the liberty of getting you a sherry Father."

"Oh no, that won't do, it is a myth that the clergy drink only sherry, I will have a large brandy Father. Be careful, they sell a brand here that doubles as brass cleaner."

"Here's to you Father, happy one hundredth birthday."

"Thank you, and to absent friends."

"Did you find your friends in the churchyard?"

"Yes, and I have my own plot reserved right next to them. Mr Hawkins does a fine job of keeping the grounds relieved of weeds and brambles, and I'm sure if he baked cakes, they would surpass his wife's. I must conclude my confession."

"There is more?"

"Yes, yes, where was I?"

"The hanging of Father Fabian."

"Oh yes, as I said, I could have stopped him, but I gave him more reason than ever, as if I had dealt the fatal blow myself. I believed Father Fabian's testimony that he shared his cell with not only a villain but also a malevolence he could not purify without an exorcism or bloodshed."

The door creaked open; Mrs Hawkins popped her head around the corner.

"Hello Fathers, I will be heading back to the rectory now."

"Let me drive you, we'll be heading that way shortly."

"I wouldn't wish to cut short your little drink Fathers."

"I am rather tired, Father Martin, and I'd like to watch the sun set over the village. If you run Mrs Hawkins back to the rectory and then drop me at the top of the hill, it's the perfect spot to watch the sun's glorious descent. I can manage to walk back with my cane, and you can head off to Cotting from there Father."

We dropped Mrs Hawkins at the rectory and proceeded to drive to the top of the hill.

"Pull in just here Father, there is a lovely spot overlooking the village. I've not seen it for many a year, the sunset and a cigarette, my guilty pleasure if you like."

"I hope you do feel some sort of absolution Father Ambrose, but I fear you have been carrying an enormous amount of unfounded guilt for the last forty-odd years."

"If that were true, then the name of Willard Adams would not haunt me so."

From beneath my gown I pulled out a collection of loose pages, two damaged and detached covers held together by a red silk ribbon and handed them to Father Martin.

"It was once a journal written by the Abbess of St Agnes', the contents are compelling if not terrifying, and if you should ever doubt my story, my rationale or your own faith, these pages will strengthen your need to continue as a man of God. Every word the abbess did scribe was true.

You remember I said I knew that face, scarred and creased, eyes that burrow into a man's soul."

"Yes, you'd seen the likes of Adams` treachery a hundred times before."

"And the gentle face of Father Fabian, my guide and mentor, all I had to do was to persuade him to make the right decision, because he only had a few days left inside those walls."

"And you did your best, Father Ambrose."

"Yes, I did, and Father Fabian carried out my plan without question or hesitation, he was fearless, sacrificing all he was, and all he knew. He took Adams` life with that humble cedar cross, and he paid the price at the end of a rope.

"Tell me this Father Martin, if you defeat the devil by taking a man's life do you not rejoice in the glory of God?"

"I fear that I cannot answer that my friend."

"Trust me, you are bound by guilt to never forget, no matter how foul a life you have ended."

"Surely that guilt did rest upon Father Fabian's conscience, he took the life of Adams and was duly judged for his act."

"But it was I who guided his hand, as if I had plunged the cross into his neck myself."

"I do acknowledge your confession, Father Ambrose, but I cannot give forgiveness, as this would just add to your suffering and guilt of a crime you did not commit."

"I do not wish for forgiveness my friend."

"Then what Father?"

"Acknowledgement, acknowledgement that it was I, along with those tattered pages that you now hold, which I also bestowed upon Father Fabian, and the unquestionable words and authority of the Abbess Sister Magdalena. It was my cross and under my express instructions that Father Fabian should kill Willard Adams. It is said that the apple does not fall far from the tree. I have lived in the hope, that it's not always true."

Father Martin looked down at the well-worn pages, bound within the detached and frayed covers of the journal, his confusion was most evident, his silence louder than any words could express.

I could see he now understood my confession, but not my motive, and that my ramblings were not the pursuit of a man in need of forgiveness or that of a priest grasping for atonement for the coercion of another, that led to Adams' murder.

"To be clear Father Martin, so there is no confusion, I am responsible for the murder of Adams and death of Father Fabian."

He opened the car door and helped me out, placed his hand on my shoulder and made the sign of the cross, he then placed the fragile journal on the seat and drove away, questioning I'm sure all that he had heard. I so wished I could tell him the whole story, but that I fear may never happen.

The evening sky was awash of reds and orange hues and the sun had started its descent. I slowly manoeuvred my way into the trees. The old path was now all but gone, overgrown bushes and tightly spaced trees hiding a once well used path. Small pockets of soft forgiving moss under foot covered the woodland floor, and as I left the canopy of the trees and brambles, there it was, that beautiful view from Valley Point, the village of Medcott below in the distance, and the darkness of Blackthorn Hill rising up to meet the burning sky.

I steered my ageing bones down to the edge of the large flat stone slab. As I looked out across the valley, I remembered Father Fabian's words. "The beauty of a setting sun, is hope enough that a new and better day will follow."

His willing gift, his sacrifice that rid the world of my father, Willard Adams, and the end of that unholy legion that found comfort within his darkness, it ends with me and fitting that the sun goes down on Blackthorn Hill. I made my way to the end of the ledge, my hands were cold and my legs were weak, the gentle breeze carried voices that drifted all around, "Go on, go on, go on Joel, closer, get closer you chicken."

It was good to hear my old name once more. I had been Father Ambrose for so long, I had forgotten the hapless Joel. I glanced to my right and there sitting a ways back, young Abner and Joseph. Faces I had forgotten, and so, I dared myself to move closer and closer to the edge.

I felt no warmth from the setting sun, and as darkness fell their faces disappeared, their voices silenced by the evening birdsong. I knew I would see them soon enough, my friends, my brothers and we would roam these hills once more, and with the beauty of that setting sun, hope enough that a new and better day would follow.